Praise for the

"*Faith and Fidelity* is truly a moving masterpiece by a gifted author. This book offers so much that it is impossible to express everything that it evokes."

-- Kimberly Spinney, *Ecataromance*

I laughed out loud, cried and laughed some more. By the end, I still had tears in my eyes from joy, the joy of reading a fantastic book. In my opinion, *Faith & Fidelity* deserves a Gold Star Award."

-- Marcy Arbitman, *Just Erotic Romance Reviews*

Love & Loyalty

"*Love & Loyalty* has a depth of emotion and a richness to the characters that comes across very well..."

– Kassa, *Rainbow Reviews*

"The characters are so incredibly three dimensional that you see their fragility and feel the emotions... Highly recommended and definitely a keeper. IMO Ms Michaels has written another winner!"

– *Reviews by Jessewave*

"*Love and Loyalty*, the sequel to *Faith and Fidelity*, is by far one of the best sequels I've read in a while. This is a fantastic story..."

– *Literary Nymphs*

Loose Id ®

ISBN 13: 978-1-60737-620-0
LOVE & LOYALTY
Copyright © May 2010 by Tere Michaels
Originally released in e-book format in September 2009

Cover Art by Croco Designs
Cover Layout by April Martinez

DISCLAIMER: Many of the acts described in our BDSM/fetish titles can be dangerous. Please do not try any new sexual practice, whether it be fire, rope, or whip play, without the guidance of an experienced practitioner. Neither Loose Id nor its authors will be responsible for any loss, harm, injury or death resulting from use of the information contained in any of its titles.

Printed in the U.S.A. by
Lightning Source, Inc.
1246 Heil Quaker Blvd
La Vergne TN 37086
www.lightningsource.com

LOVE & LOYALTY

Chapter One

James "Jim to Almost Everyone" Shea moved quickly through the throng of reporters and gawkers camped out on the front steps of the Seattle courthouse. He was quick on the heels of his partner, Terry Oh, who jogged ahead, pushing microphones and cameras out of their faces with a terse "no comment."

No comment from the detectives who had pursued Tripp Ingersoll for two years, running down every lead they could to connect the round-faced college student with the murder of a Seattle prostitute named Carmen Kelly. *No comment* after a six-week trial that had taken a toll on everyone involved.

Terry reached the front doors and gave a uniformed cop the high sign. No need to flash his badge, and Jim didn't even bother to reach into his pocket. They'd been here every day they could of the trial, and they were sure as hell expected now that the verdict would be read.

"Come on," Terry said, urging Jim in front of him. Jim felt a mix of gratitude and annoyance at the hand on his arm—he didn't like being handled, but he could use some help not exploding.

The high-profile, truTV-coverage, tabloid tone of this case drove him to distraction. High solve rates meant nothing to Jim if the guilty party didn't get put away. And this guy needed to have his moneyed, privileged ass thrown into prison for the rest of his natural life. Jim honestly didn't know what he was going to do if the verdict came down not guilty.

He knew that was wrong. He *knew* it. After almost twenty years on the force, he'd heard the speeches over and over again. He'd given them to new recruits, new detectives—hell, Terry'd gotten it a few months after joining the homicide department. You pursued the suspects, you collected the evidence, you handed over the best possible case to the prosecutor, and that was it. That was all you could do within the confines of your job.

This time, for whatever reason—the Kellys, the smug refusal of the suspect to even take them or the charges seriously—this case had dominated him emotionally. He could put the blame on a midlife crisis or burnout or some condition that middle-aged gay men got and shrinks wrote books about, but the reasons didn't matter at this point. Jim was fried, and his last shred of sanity was linked with the verdict of five women and seven men and whatever was written on that sheet of paper.

Terry got them into the courtroom without too much hassle; they exchanged nods and brief hugs with Carmen's parents, Ed and Della Kelly. Their fragile composure, the lines of grief and pain eaten into the planes of their faces—it seemed to echo what was going on in Jim's gut.

He sat down and tried to breathe.

Terry vibrated beside him, twisting his wedding ring round and round. This was his first big trial, his first experience with a case that got under your skin and squeezed your middle until you thought you might bust with the need to solve it. The newlywed wasn't having a whole lot of luck explaining this to his wife—a situation that further weighed on Jim's mind. Divorces and breakups were so common in the squad room that no one bothered to write out a card or attend a bachelor party anymore. It seemed dishonest. It was depressing, and you could pretty much guess the outcome.

It was the excuse he gave when people asked why he wasn't seeing anyone.

The courtroom filled up: curious spectators, family members from both sides, then the prosecutors and the defense lawyers. Then the moment everyone held their breath for—the entrance of Tripp Ingersoll. His parents and girlfriend leaned forward to pat his arm and sniffle sympathetically; Jim tried very hard not to hate them and remember that maybe, just maybe, they really did think he was innocent.

Because if he imagined they just didn't care or think a dead teenage prostitute, strangled and left in an empty parking lot, was worth this "inconvenience," he might explode.

Business was taken care of quickly, and Judge Crenshaw stepped out of chambers. Jim stood with his hands tightly clenched, listening to Terry huff and mutter next to him in Korean, listening to the murmurs of the gallery.

The jury was brought in. Everyone seemed to take a collective lean forward.

Jim scanned the two rows of jurors, reading their expressions as best he could, a growing sense of dread in his stomach. They weren't looking at the side of the gallery where the detectives and the Kellys were sitting. They weren't looking at the defense table, where Tripp rubbed his hands through his boyish curls and straightened the collar of his $150 silk shirt.

They were looking at Mr. and Mrs. Ingersoll and Tracey, the faithful girlfriend. And they looked relieved.

Jim swallowed hard and pressed his elbow into Terry's side as if to warn him what was going to happen. He clamped down everything—the fury, the despair, the confusion, and held his breath.

Not guilty.

The courtroom went crazy even as Judge Crenshaw banged his gavel and the deputies in the room tensed toward the crowd. Screams of joy and the weeping Mrs. Ingersoll led the rolling wave of noise as the Kellys seemed to collapse in on themselves.

Jim couldn't move. Terry broke out of a stunned stupor and began cursing under his breath. Other detectives familiar with the case rumbled behind them. A few of Carmen's childhood friends who'd come from Tacoma for the trial wept.

Quiet was restored quickly. Everyone sat down, and Jim got a perfect view of Tripp Ingersoll's smirking, joyful face as he reached over the back of his chair to hold Tracey's hand. He did it; he beat it. He'd gotten away with murder. Jim shoved down the little voice telling him that it would be worth his career to get up and take a few strides to Tripp's side and beat the ever-loving shit out of him...

But he didn't. He stayed there as Judge Crenshaw glowered and spat out the rest of the required words; clearly the judge wasn't any more delighted with the verdict than the rest of Carmen's supporters.

Then it was over.

"Come on, let's go talk to the Kellys," Terry mumbled in his ear. Jim nodded automatically, then stood up and made his way over to where the prosecutors, Nick Nathan and Heather Gomez, were trying to comfort the devastated couple.

"I'm..." Jim tried to apologize, but Mr. Kelly was already shaking his head. The man was only ten years his senior, but the number might have been a hundred at this point.

"Not your fault," he rasped, taking one hand off his weeping wife to shake first Jim's hand, then Terry's. "Thank you for trying."

Trying. *Trying.* Jim felt a wave of rage bubble up and make him light-headed. He hadn't tried—he'd succeeded. He'd found Tripp Ingersoll, he'd put evidence into Nick's and Heather's hands, he'd testified impeccably—his notes were so fucking by the book, they were *better* than the book. Everything, he'd done everything right, and now this tiny circle of white-faced and shocked people were left with nothing.

Carmen Kelly was dead, and Tripp Ingersoll was going to the best restaurant in Seattle to celebrate the verdict.

Life wasn't fair, Jim knew. But this was—this was wrong on every level.

They stood in silence; then Nick murmured something to Heather.

"Right, good idea," Heather said. "I'll have the car brought around back, and we'll get you out of here, away from the reporters."

And away from the press conference that was no doubt going to be happening, with Tripp, his family, and the lawyers pontificating about their client's proven innocence on the front steps.

Terry and Jim helped the Kellys up and shuffled them to the side door with deputies flanking them. Tiny, birdlike Della Kelly seemed on her last legs, leaning on her husband to the point where it seemed he was almost dragging her along.

It was the second before she fell that Jim started to say, "Get a doctor," and then she was on the floor, white-faced and gasping frantically for air.

* * *

Jim walked into the empty loft at half past four in the morning. He'd been gone thirty-six hours total, almost a new record.

Almost.

He peeled off his sweat-soaked suit in the kitchen, undressed down to bare skin, and shoved everything into the wastebasket under the sink, even his shoes. He wanted no reminders of this day; he had enough material for a decade of nightmares already.

Della Kelly was dead. A massive heart attack, dead in the ambulance as they flew through the streets toward the hospital. Jim was there, watched her die, watched another decade of pain appear on Ed's shoulders.

If this was the worst day—or thirty-six hours—of Jim's life, he couldn't fathom Ed's pain.

Numb, exhausted, Jim walked to the bathroom and turned on the shower. Hot. Didn't bother with cold. If he could have thrown himself into the bottom of a lobster pot of scalding water, he would have.

The smell of death and grief clung to him, oozed out of his pores. He stepped under the hot spray and leaned against the white-tiled wall. No sleep since he woke up two days ago to get ready for court. No food, just an unholy amount of black coffee and three scotches that Terry poured down his throat at the hotel bar after they got Ed Kelly settled into his room.

They were going to pick him up in the morning so he could go back to the hospital and make arrangements to get Della's body back to Tacoma.

He really didn't need help, Ed had mentioned in a dull and dead voice before he shut the door; he'd done it before with Carmen's body.

The bottled-up grief shook Jim to the core. He had never cried over a case. Never. He was a man of compassion and heart, but he never cried over his own pain, let alone someone else's.

But the hollow black spots that were now Ed Kelly's eyes—more lifeless than any corpse he'd ever examined—haunted him. Stabbed at him like knives as he imagined over and over that closing door.

He half expected to find Ed Kelly dead when he went back tomorrow.

Because if he stopped to think about it, Jim could never survive that much pain. He couldn't imagine putting into the ground the two people you loved most in the world and being the sole survivor. He couldn't fathom feeling that powerless.

He couldn't imagine loving anyone that much.

Terrifying.

Jim gasped as his skin seemed to finally register the punishing heat of the water; he blindly grabbed for the soap and cleaned himself with military precision, each lathering circle a meditative moment. *Focus, focus, shut the door on the pain, close the door on the empathy. Slam the door on the anxiety of powerlessness and the need to fix all of it.*

He couldn't bring Carmen or Della back. He couldn't put Tripp in jail. He couldn't even go beyond the boundaries of the law, because it would be against his entire framework.

He needed to find a way to deal with this, because ultimately, he was alone. There was no one to call, no one to lean on. Ben—his former roommate, his crush—was married and a few hundred miles away, content and sleeping soundly next to the person he loved.

Terry went home to his wife.

His father didn't care what he did.

His brother probably didn't even remember *what* he did.

Jim was alone. And as horrible as that felt in this moment, it was almost a relief.

Because he didn't need to worry about loss if he never bothered to love anyone.

Chapter Two

Six months later

Terry got to the squad room two hours after Jim—and still five minutes early for their shift. Polite man that he was, he didn't ever mention the early hours—or late hours, if one counted how many times Jim just didn't leave—or the sludge coffee Jim was drinking. He just sat down with his tidy Starbucks grande tea and sighed.

Jim suppressed the urge to roll his eyes.

"Morning."

"Morning," Terry said, turning on his computer. "You want my bagel? It's an onion—they got my order wrong."

Jim tilted his head until he could see around the low gray cubicle walls to Terry's desk opposite his. "Again? Third time this week. You should say something."

Terry shrugged and reached into his backpack for the brown paper bag. "They're busy; it's no big deal. I gotta watch my girlish figure, you know."

Jim took the bag and went back to his stack of paperwork with a grunt. Terry was transparent *and* about

165 pounds soaking wet, and his figure was just fine—not that Jim made a habit of mentioning that.

"Mimi wants to know if you can come for dinner Friday night. Nick and Heather are coming too."

Heterosexual Power Cabal Monthly Dinner Party—Jim's favorite. Right after root canal but slotted in just before dinner with his father in the assisted living "dining room."

"Wow, that's *this* Friday? Man, that sucks. I have a date," Jim lied, peeling the paper off the bagel.

"Uh-huh. Why don't you bring him?" Terry said almost sweetly, and Jim balled up the wax paper to toss over the divider between their cubes.

"He's shy. And he doesn't like straights." Jim talked with his mouth full to annoy Terry, then realized it annoyed him too—so he stopped.

"Dating a bigot, Jim? That does not seem your style. Oh wait—dating a person…that seems even less your style."

Jim heard the familiar chime of Terry's cell phone being opened and groaned inwardly. The chime was followed by hushed, whispered Korean; then, as expected, Jim's phone rang.

"Oh, come on now; it's too early for this," Jim groused, picking up the line. "Hey, Mimi."

There may've been a triumphant "ha" from the cubicle next door, but it was drowned out by Mimi's cheerful voice.

"If you do actually have a date on Friday, you should bring him," she said with the exaggerated patience of a kindergarten teacher. "I can pretend to be enthralled by

Heather's breasts if that helps establish a more gay-friendly vibe."

Despite himself, Jim laughed. "She does have excellent breasts…"

Mimi snickered. "Even gay men notice breasts—why *is* that?"

"I don't know. I'll call the Gay Council and let you know."

"Good, you can tell me the results on Friday."

"Mimi…"

"*James.* You have to come when I tell you who the fourth couple is."

"I'm almost afraid to ask."

"Ben and Liddy are driving down for the weekend to visit her parents, so they'll be there. It's supposed to be a surprise for you, but I'm changing my tactics because you're being impossible. So bring wine and some beer, and let me know if your date is a vegan."

Ben, his ex-roommate and "best friend." The guy he had a long-standing, unrequited, nonreturned, intense crush on. Of course he and his new wife would be the fourth couple! Jim had that sort of luck these days.

"Well, I can't say no now," Jim said, feigning excitement. "I'll be there, and I promise to pretend to be surprised."

"Great; thank you, James," Mimi said, clearly feeling triumphant. "We're having sushi and tempura."

"What's that you said? Steak and lobster?"

"Is your date vegan?"

"You're funny, you know that?"

"Is your date *real?*"

"Bye, Mimi. I have to go now. Some of us work for a living." He ignored her last question and made kissy sounds over the line until she said something rude in Korean and hung up.

"Your wife curses like a sailor," he called to Terry.

"It's hot, isn't it?"

* * *

Jim hadn't really been on a date in over a year.

It had actually been longer since he'd been on a second date.

Blowjobs in bar bathrooms didn't really count, particularly when you didn't even bother to exchange names. And he was okay with that, seriously. Bringing someone back to the loft hadn't been a regular habit ever; he'd lived with a few boyfriends in the early days when he thought about having a relationship. He'd lived with a few straight roommates when dating got a little too intense for him; balancing work and a boyfriend was never his strong suit.

After the misadventure of having Ben live there for five years (great roommate, great friend, straight as a level—of course Jim had fallen for him), Jim had given up on roommates as well. He was considering a cat, since, like Jim, they generally seemed to be able to mete out affection, then go their own way.

Even his last random one-night stand turned weird—New York City for a conference, nice guy in a bar, good sex...and emotionally stripping. Hell, he'd even kept in touch with Matt, not hoping for more, but just enjoying his "happily ever after" in a slightly masochistic fashion.

That wasn't real bright, as nice as Matt was, as nice as it was to hear all the stuff with his boyfriend, Evan, and Evan's kids and renovating a house and basically an entire life plan that Jim couldn't even wrap his brain around existing in reality.

It managed to be life-affirming and depressing at the same time.

His friends couldn't understand it, and they told him that all the time. "*You're so nice! You're so good-looking! You're too good a guy to be alone! Want to meet my brother/neighbor/cousin/ex?*"

Mimi was the hands-down worst. After the cluster fuck that was the Ingersoll trial, she seemed to take "cop's wife" as a holy vow instead of packing her bags to return home. Gone were the phone calls to Terry asking when he'd be home; instead she showed up with dinner (or lunch or breakfast) and exuded patience. In addition to giving Terry some extra leeway, she decided Jim needed some caretaking, and off she went.

He needed a man, a proper boyfriend with good intentions and a job and a bunch of other things she felt Jim needed/deserved. It was a *long* list. Bringing a guy to the Cabal Dinner Party was out of the question; Mimi was a kick-ass cook and a first-rate interrogator and would have them applying for a civil union by the time she served dessert.

Numerous times Jim had politely suggested she consider a career in law enforcement or perhaps loan-sharking.

Now he was punching in the numbers to the vending machine, his eyes on a Snickers bar, and trying to come up with a good excuse for Friday when he turned up solo.

"Hey, Jim?" He turned around at the sound of his name and saw Heather Gomez hurrying down the hall in his direction.

"Hey, Heather." Jim reached down for his candy bar and tried not to remember discussing her breasts with Mimi. "Everything okay?"

"Oh yeah, everything's fine. Just, you know—a thousand things to do and not enough hours." She smiled, shifting her overpacked briefcase from one hand to another. "I was just wondering if you got a call from Ed Kelly."

"Recently? No, I haven't. Is he all right?"

"I'm guessing so—it didn't sound urgent or anything. He left a message for Nick as well. I thought you'd be on the list too." She smiled sadly, her eyes sympathetic behind her squared-off glasses. "Nice man, I just wish there was more we could have done for him."

It wasn't Heather's fault, of course. Or Nick's. It was no one's fault, which is what Jim told himself in the middle of the night when he couldn't sleep. No one's fault but Tripp Ingersoll.

"You and me both." Jim opened his Snickers and offered her a bite, which she shook off with a laugh.

"No, thanks, I have a wedding dress to fit into." The trial had yielded a nice side note—Nick finally got off his sorry ass and proposed to his girlfriend of seven years.

"Pft, you look great." *Particularly your breasts.* "Thanks for the heads-up about Ed Kelly. I'll check my messages."

They made a few more seconds of small talk. Heather brought up Friday's dinner party, and Jim dragged his ass back to his desk with the Snickers in his teeth.

There was indeed a voice mail from Ed Kelly on Jim's cell. His reedy voice was calm and centered; he needed to talk to Jim about something regarding Carmen's case—he needed some advice. That was all after a recitation of Ed's number, which Jim knew by heart. Jim played it three times, searching for a small indication of what this was about. Maybe the civil case? A few people had encouraged Ed to sue Tripp Ingersoll for damages, but Ed wasn't interested. He'd had enough of Ingersoll and courtrooms for his lifetime, he said. Besides—the money wouldn't bring back Carmen or Della.

All offers from talk-show hosts and pseudojournalists had gone unanswered. Ed was never interested in sitting down with Katie Couric or Oprah. Hollywood got the same cold slammed door. Ed was a man who could not be bought.

Jim gave Ed's home number a dial, tapping a pencil against the desk anxiously. The machine clicked on after a few rings, and Jim gnawed on his lip.

"Hey, Ed, it's Jim. I got your message, giving you a call back. Call my cell, okay? I'll make sure I pick up."

He hung up and contemplated the endless pile of case files on his desk. More dead mothers, fathers, sons, daughters. More grieving families who never recovered. The endless cycle of violence that surrounded Jim every hour of every day.

Sometimes he wondered what the hell the point was.

Chapter Three

"Take a left up here...where it says Oak Street. Right, the street you just passed? That would be Oak."

Griffin Drake rolled his eyes as his driving companion, Daisy Baylor, crinkled the printed-out directions. The rental car had no GPS, and neither of them had the best navigation skills in the world. He walked a lot, and she, glamorous actress that she was, was driven everywhere—by trained professionals with GPS...and most likely a sense of direction.

But here they were, lost in Tacoma—note to self, he thought as he found a driveway to U-turn in, that's a great title—trying to make a meeting with a very important man named Ed Kelly. Griffin didn't want to be late, not for this, and he didn't want to hear Daisy pointing out his supreme lack of driving skills, which would probably end with them "lost in Canada."

"Okay—left on Oak..."

"No! Right on Oak; we're backward now!"

"You ain't whistling Dixie, Daisy Mae," he muttered, lifting his sunglasses so he could squint and see the rusted-over street sign.

Oak. Right.

"I think I'm overdressed." Daisy fretted next to him, smoothing a Paris original over her knees. She would move to playing with her hair next; then, if they didn't get there in the next five minutes, he'd be talking her out of a cigarette. Then talking himself out of joining her. New Year's resolutions sounded a lot easier when you were drunk and hanging out on the roof of a millionaire director's mansion as opposed to, say, driving to a pitch that could make or break your future career path.

"You look incredible, and I'm guessing he won't be able to name the designer or price tag on your dress, so we're good." Although they did want Ed Kelly to know they were good for the funding—in a subtle way. That was important.

"Okay, that was a quarter mile—where should we be now?"

"Left on Mill, right on Percy; then it's the fifth house." Daisy focused on the directions and not her outfit, which was good for Griffin. They'd known each other for over twenty-five years, and for some reason it never got easier to be anxious at the same time.

One at a time? Usually her. He handled it like a pro. It was practically his full-time job after screenwriting. At the same time? Someone call a shrink and a bartender, stat.

He had the speech in his head, how he was going to pitch this movie idea to Mr. Kelly, how they wanted his and Della and Carmen's story to be heard without the background sensationalism. How he was going to point out the good things that could be done with his share of the profits—a scholarship, a community garden. Anything he wanted. It didn't have to be for *him*. He just needed to keep it simple, honest and sincere—and not tip his hand about just how important it all was to him and Daisy.

He knew Ed Kelly's story from the press surrounding the trial and a few sympathetic pieces in the local and national papers. The man who lost so much but refused to seek revenge or restitution or sell his story. It was the story of a man who could have been someone who lived down the street from Griffin's family—a man living in a run-down house in a lower-middle-class suburb with seemingly nothing to show for his life except an inner peace most people would kill for. Or were currently spending thousands of dollars trying to find through psychics or pills or retreats to ashrams.

Words like "scoop" and "coup" didn't even touch how badly Hollywood wanted Ed Kelly's story, hyped and heightened, of course, mostly because the man was so damn untouchable. In a world of selling your story as the paramedics were cutting a shark off your leg, this guy wouldn't even return phone calls.

But he returned Daisy and Griffin's call. *They* were in possession of his home address and were expected at this moment. Something about their letter intrigued him, pulled him to respond. Griffin was still giddy about the whole thing.

By the time Daisy announced, "Here, right here," Griffin felt sure his appeal would be accepted. They would do this.

Griffin shut off the car and gave Daisy a pat on the shoulder. She blazed that internationally famous smile in his direction, adjusted her sunglasses, and opened the door with a forceful push.

"Hey, there's someone else here, I think," Daisy said, eyeing the second pickup truck in the dirt driveway. The one closest to the house had seen better days, rusty but pin neat. The second was a giant black Chevy Silverado, all gleaming and authoritative like a sentry.

"Not even a whimsical bumper sticker," Daisy said drily, hoisting her handbag over her shoulder.

"I wouldn't want to bump into that thing while I'm on my motorcycle," Griffin pointed out, hurrying to catch up.

"If you did, I'd be writing the eulogy for your funeral." Taking his hand, she walked up the creaky wooden stairs to the screen door.

"I'm sure you'd do a lovely job. Do they give Emmys for eulogies?"

"Shut up, or I'll sic that truck on you."

"Wonder who it is," he whispered, coming up behind her. Even in her platforms she still only came up to his shoulder. He resisted the urge to pat the top of her head.

"Lawyer?"

"In a pickup truck?"

"It's *Tacoma*."

Daisy knocked on the door, peering through the screen door into the dark house.

Griffin heard men's voices from inside, and then out of the dark came a very tall, imposing figure, and he knew in one that wasn't Ed Kelly.

The "might be a lawyer" guy was broad-shouldered and on alert, just a silhouette of aggression behind the strained screen. And he wasn't opening the door.

"Hi," Daisy said brightly. "We have an appointment with Mr. Kelly. Ms. Baylor and Mr. Drake."

From the military haircut to the well-worn jeans, Griffin guessed their mystery man was less a lawyer and more a man who knew his way around a gun. A cop, maybe? Some of the articles on Kelly and the trial mentioned a few detectives he'd gotten very close to.

"You're one of the detectives from Carmen's trial," Griffin said boldly, going to the top step to match the other man's height—and glare. "I was thinking that Mr. Kelly would probably give you a call."

The bullshit, "pulled out of his ass" bluff worked, and the man nodded, reaching for the door handle.

"Detective Shea," he said, taking a step back and gesturing them in.

"Griffin Drake and Daisy Baylor. Pleasure." Griffin quickly extended his hand, trying to keep the upper hand on Detective Shea.

"Ed called me up, told me about this meeting. I decided to be here for him." Detective Shea shook Griffin's hand firmly, then reached for Daisy's; she just stared at him, and Griffin knew she was thinking, *Boy, this guy is hot.*

Because they always had the same taste in men.

"And we can certainly appreciate that," Daisy piped up, suddenly finding her movie-star manners. "I think it's really incredible that you're still around for him."

Something crossed over Detective Shea's impressive face—something like grief or guilt, and Griffin toed his boot into the heavy linoleum of the entryway.

"He's a good guy. I want to make sure people don't take advantage of him," Detective Shea said quietly. The glower had dimmed, but the warning was clear.

"Bring 'em in, Jim; I think you scared 'em enough," a voice called from the next room, and the detective's exterior cracked slightly.

Griffin had his hand at Daisy's back, letting her take the lead. People loved Daisy, whether it was on the big screen or in line at the supermarket. She just batted her eyelashes and made everyone adore her.

He referred to it as her "don't club me, said the baby seal" look on more than one occasion. He'd also rode that look and her D-cups into a fairly decent career, so Griffin tried not to mock it too much.

Mr. Kelly was seated in a seventies-era recliner, wearing old jeans and a plaid shirt, glasses perched on his nose. From his notes, Griffin knew Mr. Kelly was a decade younger than his own father back in Albany, but he might as well have been thirty years older. The toll the past few years had taken on him was painful and obvious, as the man was even more gaunt than the pictures from the trial showed.

"Mr. Kelly, thank you so much for seeing us," Daisy said, extending her hand.

"Pleasure, Miss Baylor." The man seemed to blush a little in the dimly lit room as he stood up to shake her hand. "I seen a bunch of your films. Carmen was a big fan of yours—I think that's probably why I thought I'd give you a listen."

Daisy didn't miss a beat. She gave Mr. Kelly a little hug, then stepped back, embarrassed. "Sorry. I do that sometimes."

"I'm not gonna turn down a hug from a movie star." Ed Kelly laughed. He reached around to offer his hand to Griffin. "Mr. Drake, you gonna hug me too?"

"Maybe after you buy me a drink." Griffin coughed as the line slid out of his mouth, but it seemed to further break the ice. Even the sentry, Detective Shea, had to smile. A tiny smile that might've been a facial tic, but still—he hadn't pulled a gun on them yet, so that was a good thing.

Ed Kelly seated them on a quilt-covered couch, then sat back in his recliner. The detective disappeared into another room, and from the clanging sounds it appeared to be a kitchen.

"We got coffee, tea if you want it. Lipton, hope that's okay. Jim brought up some cookies from this fancy-pants bakery in Seattle."

"You didn't have to go through so much trouble," Daisy said, laying her purse near her feet.

"Movie star in my house? Heck, I even vacuumed."

Daisy giggled and did the "oh you" hand gesture that men of Ed Kelly's generation fell for like a redwood at the mercy of an ax. Griffin managed to roll his eyes while he reached into his pocket for his BlackBerry for compulsive e-mail check number seven since they'd left the airport.

Detective Shea—Jim—reappeared with a fancy silver tray full of mismatched coffee cups, a decanter, and a plate of cookies. He looked to Griffin like a very large, cranky yet attractive waiter.

Like…Lurch at Tavern on the Green.

* * *

There was small talk about the drive up to Ed's house, traffic, weather, Hollywood traffic and weather, and where everyone was from originally. Griffin tried to get away with "the East Coast," but Daisy loved to tell stories about them as kids at performing arts camp in the Adirondacks, which ate up a cup of coffee, one refill, six cookies, and almost forty minutes of Griffin Drake's life.

Griffin wanted to get to his pitch, but Daisy seemed bent on making Ed Kelly's day, and the more she did that, the more Ed relaxed, the more Jim Shea eased out of red alert.

So Griffin kept his mouth shut.

Until there was a lull in conversation and Jim Shea looked straight over to Griffin, a Local 458 mug tight in his hand.

"You came here to ask Ed to sell his story," he said bluntly, his eyes narrowing. "You know you're not the first people to have tried."

This was it. Gauntlet thrown down. He wasn't in a fancy LA office, he wasn't at a trendy restaurant, or even throwing down his pitch in the elevator of a hotel at Sundance. This was as real life as he'd gotten in a very long time, and his usual tap dance didn't fit here.

So he went to the sincere pitch he'd been practicing for months.

"We're the first people to get into his living room," Griffin said, just as bluntly, giving Ed Kelly a sidelong apologetic look.

"I won't insult anyone by pretending this isn't about a movie and us making money. I won't give Mr. Kelly a speech about doing this for a higher cause. But I'm thinking telling Carmen's side of the story, telling Ed's side of the story—that's not a bad thing to want. The trial didn't tell the full story. The press hasn't gotten a full picture.

"And"—Griffin took a deep breath, turning to Ed, his face deadly serious—"I know you don't want to make money off this. I understand that. If I were in your position, I'd tell me to shove my money where the sun don't shine, because it won't change anything. But...but I'm thinking you're a good-hearted man, and you could do something with the money. Something...that's the right sort of legacy for Carmen and Della."

Sweat crept up under Griffin's collared shirt and prickled his forehead. He imagined he could hear a pin drop in between the clicks and ticks of the mantel clock.

He clasped his hands, dropped his gaze to the gold, matted rug under his feet. Please, he thought, please give me this chance.

Ed Kelly cleared his throat and took a sip of his coffee, the side of the cup reading *Number 1 Dad*. Suddenly Griffin wasn't sure if he was proud of himself for trying to pull this deal off, or if he was a rampaging asshole for even opening his mouth. It was a total toss-up at that moment.

"I don't want nothing on the screen that would have embarrassed Della," he said simply, his voice quiet and cracking. "No naked stuff and not a lot of swearin'. And I'd like to read your script before you go on and start the filming stuff. And..." Mr. Kelly was on a roll. "And Jim reads it too, so none of the cops or the prosecutors look bad."

Griffin wanted to jump and dance on the couch, but he held his composure perfectly. Could it really be this easy? "You have my word this script will be what you're looking for. And we don't want to make anyone look bad, Mr. Kelly—no one deserves that."

Except for Tripp Ingersoll, but Griffin wasn't going to say the name out loud.

"Okay, then. You got lawyers, I suppose." Ed looked over at Jim, who hadn't said a word yet. "I should get me a lawyer too."

"I'll call my friend Ben. He and his wife have a small practice not too far from here. They'll take care of whatever you need."

"Perfect. You trust 'em, I trust 'em."

"Oh my gosh, we're going to do this," Daisy said suddenly, then covered her mouth as her inside voice went to the outside. "You won't regret this, Mr. Kelly; I promise you that from the bottom of my heart."

"I'm holding you to that, young lady." He gestured toward Griffin with his cup. "You too, young man. I don't have much of a temper, but Jim here..." He let his voice drift off, a smile playing on his lips. "He's a hell of a watchdog."

Jim made an embarrassed sound as Daisy clapped her hands. "Okay, that's it—hugs all around." She got up and gave Ed a squeeze in his recliner.

She sidestepped Jim as one would a hungry mountain lion and threw her arms around Griffin.

"We did it," she murmured in his ear. "The first step, we took it."

Griffin watched Jim over Daisy's shoulder as he gave her a celebratory hug. Those cool blue eyes were echoing Ed Kelly's joking words—if they fucked this up, Jim Shea was going to take a bite out of both of them, and not in a good way.

Chapter Four

Jim had driven up to Tacoma after taking a last-minute vacation day; he had about seventy-four years' worth built up, so one day wasn't going to kill him. Of course, that meant getting out of the Heterosexual Cabal Dinner with surprise guests Ben and Liddy. But everyone gave him a pass when they heard this was about Ed and some potentially sharklike Hollywood assholes who wanted to make a movie about Ed's ordeal after Carmen's murder.

He promised Ben he'd stop by their new house the next weekend. He swore to Mimi he'd make next month's Friday night Power Dinner. He made a lot of promises he knew he'd have to keep before he'd jumped in his truck and headed for Tacoma.

Everyone thought it was proof of Jim's excellent character that he did so much for Ed. Visits, calls, money— only Terry and Jim's accountant knew about the money— whatever the other man needed, Jim took care of. He even had a local handyman on his speed dial who'd run over to take care of things so Ed didn't have to.

Jim didn't mind carrying the burdens. Ed had a lot; he could use the help. Others did what they could, but Ed's trust of Jim extended into areas beyond baskets of food and monthly check-up phone calls.

Jim knew Ed was dying.

Insult upon injury, the life of Job. An exam a few months ago revealed Ed had advanced pancreatic cancer, and the only person outside of his doctor who knew was Jim.

Along with the prognosis, Jim knew where Ed's will was, what funeral home he wanted to be handled by, and where the deed to the plot where Della and Carmen were buried was kept. During the last visit they'd discussed what Jim would do with the house and the truck.

Ed dealt with the whole thing matter-of-factly. In the grand scheme of life, it wasn't the worst thing that ever happened to him.

Jim met his realism with his own brand of protective stoicism. They were quite the pair, that was for sure.

Sometimes Jim wondered if it wasn't misplaced guilt, not just over being unable to see justice served but his own issues with his father, who lived in Vancouver in an upscale nursing home with around-the-clock care and the best of everything—provided by strangers.

Or maybe guilt he hadn't done more to put Tripp Ingersoll in jail. Or just killed him some night, weeks after the trial; old-fashioned vigilante justice with Jim pleading temporary insanity. He knew, with shame and sureness, that if Ed had asked or given permission, he could have done it.

So it was a lot to do with guilt, his relationship with Ed. Too many shades to put a label on.

* * *

The writer and the actress were nice, almost too nice. Daisy Baylor was a bona fide movie star—even Jim had seen her in a few things, and he only went to the movies... Well, he never went to the movies—all shiny gorgeous with perfect, tumbling red curls and a dress he suspected cost more than all four of his last snow tires put together. She was affectionate and kind to Ed, and Jim watched him light up for the first time in...possibly for the first time ever.

The only thing that came close was when Ed got into the occasional melancholy mood and decided to talk about Carmen and Della. Jim suspected that Daisy Baylor reminded Ed a bit of Della in her heyday, the years before things got ugly, with Carmen getting into trouble and eventually running away. That, combined with the advancing of the cancer, no doubt put into Ed's mind that he wanted to make this deal now.

Jim understood, but he didn't like it.

The writer—Drake—had the right pitch. It was the perfect note to hit with Ed. It made Jim suspicious. All that honesty? That earnestness? That pleading note to his voice? Must be fake. Must be.

He was also handsome in a geeky sort of way; Jim suspected a sharp sense of humor under all that preppy showcasing. He also knew with dreaded certainty if they met in a bar that Griffin Drake would be one of those nameless blowjobs. Unfortunately, they'd met in the real world, and Jim just wrote him off as someone to be watched—carefully.

After they left, Jim and Ed sat for a few hours speculating on how this process would go down. Jim wanted to argue the point, but then Ed—as Ed was prone to do—dropped the latest bombshell in Jim's lap.

"You're gonna be the executor of my will and all, so those legal papers your friends draw up—they need to say that when I'm not here, you're the one who's my voice in this movie. You make sure they do right by everyone."

And Jim—as Jim was prone to do—didn't put up a fight or protest as his stomach did a roller-coaster bump.

* * *

Monday morning Jim was back at his desk, late for him. It was almost six a.m. He didn't remember sleeping all that much in the past thirty-six hours, except for a brief nap on Ed Kelly's couch. There was food interspersed in there and a shower before he headed into the station with a gallon or so of coffee in his gut. He figured he'd be good for ten-or-so hours—then he'd probably hit a wall and collapse in the break room.

The squad room was quiet; a few phones rang on and off, hushed conversations drifted above the cubicles. Jim checked his calendar and realized two things—his birthday was two weeks away, and Captain Hedges's retirement was tomorrow.

Which meant ironing his dress blues.

And then spending the next two weeks avoiding any attempts by his friends to celebrate his birthday.

Jim sighed. Forty-five. Really? Already? The last birthday he recalled with any type of clarity was his twenty-first. His father gave him the legal papers to his grandfather's inheritance over a stiff, expensive meal at a French restaurant. Then his friends—mostly his compatriots on the football team and his roommate, whom he was also secretly dating—took him to Vegas for enough debauchery that even today he wondered if he should just arrest himself on several counts. Public drunkenness, gambling, and a lot of sex with his boyfriend in their hotel room when everyone else had gone off to find some hookers. God, that had been a great birthday because he was young and hot and rich, independent of his father, and didn't have a care in the world.

Forty-five looked incredibly different and very depressing.

"Hey, Detective Shea, there's a package for you down at the desk," a uniformed cop walking by broke his reverie. "You want me to bring it up?"

"Is it ticking?" Jim was only half joking.

"No." The young cop laughed, pausing to lean on the cubicle wall. He gave Jim a once-over and a more flirtatious smile, and Jim felt *old*. Older than dirt, actually. Back in his early uniform days, you'd never even consider flirting publicly with another cop—particularly not in the squad room. "It's not a problem, really."

"It's okay, I'll get it." Jim looked down at his desk, trying to shuffle papers in an attempt to look busy.

"All right. I'll talk to you later." The cop lingered, then walked away slowly.

It was like a bar. Only fully lit and, you know, *work*. Jim's hands shook a little. His sexual orientation was generally known and generally not a problem. In liberal, godless Seattle, being a bigot or homophobe is what you held close to your chest—not being gay. All his partners had known; none had ever asked for a transfer. Terry Oh had been "schooled" on his first day and just politely assured Jim he was straight and engaged but would be flattered if Jim wanted to check him out when he wasn't looking. Everyone knew. But no one said anything. No one came on to him. He knew other gay and lesbian cops on the force; there were no meetings or weekly dinners where they had meaningful conversations on being gay and blue.

Jim didn't like to cross streams like that. He didn't like being hit on by a twentysomething who had no clue what it was like to be afraid.

He forgot to be flattered the guy was interested.

* * *

Terry arrived with yet another "mistake" onion bagel, plopping it on Jim's desk without a word.

"How'd the thing at Ed's go? You scare off the Hollywood freaks?" Terry sipped his latte, leaning against the cubicle wall exactly where the flirter had been.

"Actually…" Jim sighed, pushing his chair back and testing how far he could lean without hearing a squeak. "Ed accepted their deal."

"No shit!" Terry looked shocked. "You let him?"

"What was I going to do?" Jim swallowed the information about Ed's health. "They were like, all sincere and nice, and you know who the actress was? Daisy Baylor."

Terry almost swallowed his tongue. "Holy crap, Jim. Daisy Baylor?" His pale skin pinkened. "She's totally on my list."

"List?"

"You know, the list you have of the people your wife or husband would let you sleep with if you got the chance—no penalties."

"Straight people are crazy."

"Is she as hot in person as she was in *The Betrayed Night?* Because she was..." Terry's voice trailed off. "Seriously."

Jim tried to remember that one. He thought it was the one where she was naked a lot and cried.

"She looks like a normal person until you remember normal people aren't that perfect." Jim shook his head. "The screenwriter guy is apparently some childhood friend of hers, and they're making this movie for like...Sundance or something." Jim shrugged. He'd rather watch the Military or History Channel. "Artsy, I guess. I gotta read the script— make sure they don't shit on you and me and Heather and Nick."

Terry's jaw actually dropped. "We're going to be in it?

"I guess characters who're supposed to be us. You'll probably get some paperwork at some point, asking permission."

"Will Daisy Baylor deliver the paperwork?"

"I'm calling Mimi, you perv."

* * *

It was after lunchtime before Jim remembered the package at the front desk. He and Terry finished some meatloaf specials over at the corner diner, and he stopped on his way back upstairs to ask Sergeant Filipano for his box.

They bullshitted about the retirement festivities tomorrow, people they knew, and then Jim was hoisting a mildly heavy rectangle in his hands. As he stepped into the elevator, he realized the return address was Hollywood.

Were legal papers this heavy?

At his desk he took a pocketknife to the cardboard and flipped the cover off; it wasn't legal papers.

It was coffee and fancy cookies, plus some books on Washington State history. A gray envelope sat on top, and Jim opened the flap. The folded paper inside smelled girly sweet, but the writing was masculine.

Detective Shea,

Daisy and I just wanted to say thank you for your help.

As we told you and Mr. Kelly, we have the best possible intentions for this project. We're looking forward to working with you.

Best,

Griffin Drake

Jim poked through the package. It was…thoughtful. Put together as opposed to ordered off a Web site. Neatly packed in the box by an assistant, no less, but still—Jim was mildly impressed.

Then he went back to remembering not to trust these people.

Chapter Five

Griffin Drake and his MacBook were the best of friends, more intimate than lovers. He slept with it. He cared for it with specially made cleaning cloths and cans of air to keep it dust free. Plants and fish had died under his watch with alarming regularity, but the computer—the computer was tended like a child.

Now, in the middle of devoting all his time to the Ed Kelly script, Griffin was toting the laptop around his West Hollywood neighborhood. To the park for a few hours, to the coffee store for lunch and a few hours more, mainlining coffee and unsuccessfully resisting the freshly baked macaroons. To the front steps of his condo, where he again opened the blank document and stared.

Nothing. Not a goddamn word. He couldn't even come up with a title beyond "The Ed Kelly Script."

So he scored the coup of the year in terms of subject and then forgot how to write. Maybe there was a script in that. A black comedy, clearly.

Utterly defeated, Griffin fiddled around in his pocket and got out his keys, juggling the precious laptop. It wasn't her fault how badly he sucked as a writer. Really.

For twelve years he'd been one of the very few writers who made a decent living in screenwriting. No television, no books, no ghostwriting—just screenplays, and all fifteen he'd written (or rewritten) were made.

In this business, it was almost unheard of unless you had an "in." Which Griffin did, to his credit and shame: Daisy Mae's Deal with the Devil—also known as her marriage to Claus—which had propelled them out of New York state, past college graduation, and straight to the hallowed halls of employment at a giant Hollywood studio. Not to mention he could write blow 'em up, shoot 'em down, screwing in an alley to box-office perfection, and had. All fifteen of his movies involved a lot of cursing, an inventory of creative ways to kill people, and at least two tit shots per reel.

It wasn't pretty, but it was lucrative for the studio and for him.

Paid for his nice condo here and his nice condo in Aspen. Paid for his dad's house back in Albany and two nieces going to college. Paid for nice threads and gym memberships and vacations and security; he wasn't going to end up selling real estate or making porn, thank you very much. Griffin Drake was a writer and a good one, and he wasn't done yet.

Ed Kelly's movie was the next step, the higher place. The time when someone, somewhere was finally going to throw around his name and "Academy Award" in the same sentence, and not the one where a critic had complimented the scene in *Fire Water* where The Rock killed some Euro baddie with an Oscar statuette.

No, he was going to write a killer script, a heart tugger, a movie that had people discussing the life of this man and his terrible luck and his ability to keep going. Then Daisy would produce it, and they would be out from under the firm hand of Claus Miller and Bright Side Studios—quite possibly the least aptly named studio in the world.

Daisy was tired of flashing her tits, and Griffin was tired of writing scripts where she did just that.

This was their big chance.

Now if only Griffin could write one single goddamn word of it.

He kicked the door shut behind him and threw his keys onto the couch. Outside didn't help, being around people didn't help. His usual haunts weren't working. Maybe their mojo only extended to the car chases and half-naked girls appearing for no good reason that he usually hacked out for a living.

Right now he had nothing, not even an outline—just a timeline of events and every damn article ever written about the case.

It wasn't enough. He needed some connection, some viewpoint into Ed Kelly and Carmen and Della and the case. He was almost too close, feeling the middle-class values gone wrong and the muddled confusion of parents who didn't understand why their best efforts dovetailed into a teenage daughter who hooked up with the wrong people and ran away from home before her seventeenth birthday.

He knew those girls. But he couldn't seem to connect his knowledge to the story.

Jim Shea, Lurch at Tavern on the Green, überdetective, popped into his mind.

He'd gotten a polite thank-you e-mail for the "make nice" package Daisy had insisted they send. The law firm his friends worked at had taken care of Ed's side of the paperwork quickly; everything they'd asked of the other side happened. He briefly tried to imagine shooting the shit with Detective Shea about the case but got distracted by the way he looked in a dress shirt.

Griffin picked up his glove and baseball, pacing around his desk. He got a certain vibe from the detective from their first meeting. Daisy's gaydar was better than his, and she confirmed he and Griffin batted for the same team on their drive back from Ed Kelly's Tacoma home.

What could it hurt? A little flirting, a little convo—maybe it would push him out of this ridiculous slump he was in.

He reached for his phone and wedged it between his shoulder and ear after dialing Detective Jim Shea's cell phone.

Was it too early? Too late? Lunchtime? Was he on a crime scene? Was he going to be irritated by the call? Oh shit, Griffin thought, almost throwing the phone down before he was thwarted by the sound of a gruff "Jim Shea."

"Detective Shea, Griffin Drake—hope I'm not bothering you," he said, clearing his throat.

"Uh. No, you're not bothering me." The tone didn't change at all, no difference to help Griffin discern if the detective was going to call him names and hang up or be chatty. "Can I help you with something?"

"Well, I'm writing today, trying to get the script in shape for you and Mr. Kelly to read," he lied, tossing the ball in the air and catching it with a flick of his wrist. "I had a few questions, but you know, now that I'm thinking about it, I'm on LA-screenwriter time and you're on…guy-with-a-real-job time."

A sound came through the line—it might have been the detective's version of a laugh.

"I can call you back maybe, later," Jim said begrudgingly. "Seven or eight." He sighed. "Honestly, I don't know when I'm going to be home."

"You gotta eat at some point, right?" Griffin felt a brainstorm welling up. Feeling stilted, needing some inspiration—a flight from LA to Seattle was practically a hop, skip, and a jump. "I'll take you out for a late dinner."

"Uhhhh…" Detective Shea was clearly at a loss of words.

"I can be there about nine." Griffin opened his computer and went to his bookmarked travel site. "I'm guessing you'll be at your desk at least that late."

"I—Are you serious? You're flying here tonight to have dinner with me?"

"Yeah. I need some information, you need dinner." A few clicks later and Griffin was booking a flight. "Nine o'clock, nine thirty at the latest."

"Uh…okay. Sure." Jim Shea was so off his cool that Griffin almost felt sorry for him, except where he didn't because it made his ego feel good.

"Great, see you then."

Griffin hung up before Jim could regain his equilibrium.

* * *

By the time Griffin went to the airport, there was actually almost an outline. While none of his usual tricks were working, four minutes with Jim Shea on the phone helped him focus a bit better. That and spending a bit of time on Google researching the illustrious life and times of James Michael Edward Shea, with his fancy-pants lineage, military honors, and several Officer of the Year awards under his belt.

Griffin was impressed and a little intimidated. His own family were no slouches, but no one who Googled them would come up with anything beyond some obituaries and wedding announcements. The Drakes of Albany, New York, generally got birthed, married, reproduced, and died while staying in blue-collar jobs for most of their working lives.

Only Griffin had decided to leave. His father was confused enough by his only son (after eight daughters, he really had no clue what to do with a boy, let alone a gay one) but proud. He faithfully saw all Griffin's films in the movie theater and bought them on DVD, even though Griffin told him he could get them for free. He put clips from *Variety* and *Entertainment Weekly* that mentioned Griffin's name or movies on the fridge along with pictures of the grandchildren and whatever flyer for whatever fund-raiser car wash was coming up at the local schools.

Griffin, the oddity. Griffin, the gay screenwriter who lived in Hollywood.

Griffin, the guy on the plane in his best jeans and a white collared shirt and shit-kicking boots and some gel in his unruly brown hair. He put in his contacts. He threw clothes in an overnight bag, brought his computer, and didn't buy a return ticket.

He was treating this like a date. Ballsy in a way he wasn't, usually. He sincerely doubted Detective Jim Shea was going to be interested, but it was nice to pretend.

* * *

Griffin grabbed a cab at the airport, checking his BlackBerry for messages and texts and other distractions as nerves descended. Really? Seriously? Giant cop whom he's working with, flying to Seattle for *dinner?* Where the hell was this coming from? A potential taste of freedom from Bright Side's stun collar and he was suddenly jetting (okay, using miles for business class) north for wining and dining.

This was so Daisy's territory.

He dialed her cell number, watching Seattle speed by from the backseat.

His knee jiggled nervously.

His palms—sweating.

"Helllooo—where are you?" Daisy's familiar voice came through the line. From the loopy trill, she'd started the evening cocktail therapy early.

"Seattle."

"Well, I wasn't expecting that answer. What's going on? There isn't trouble with the movie, is there?" Panic seeped into her voice; they'd kept things under wraps from Bright Side so far, but nothing was guaranteed in this business, especially secrecy.

"No, no. I just—I was a little blocked, and I thought I would call Detective Shea and…"

Daisy erupted into giggles.

"Why is this funny?" Griffin scowled at his reflection in the cab's window.

"You know, I get he's hot and that whole manly macho thing you find so appealing, but flying to Seattle? That's a hell of a booty call."

"We're going to talk about the movie. Over dinner."

"Uh-huuuuuh."

"We need him on our side, Daisy; we need him on board with this movie, or Ed Kelly will pull out. You know this." Since he couldn't convince himself, convincing her was not going to happen. But he'd go down with the ship protesting that this wasn't a booty call.

"I know. But is sleeping with him now a good idea?"

"Oh come on! It's dinner. You met him—I'm guessing he's not a first-date drop-trou sort of—"

"You said date! You said date!"

"I'm hanging up now."

"Wear a condom, and please be good in the sack—if you suck, he's going to be bitter, and we can't afford that." She giggled, then hung up in a flurry of kisses.

The cab pulled up in front of the police station, and Griffin smacked his forehead against the window.

No pressure.

Chapter Six

Today was Jim Shea's forty-fifth birthday.

The Heterosexual Power Cabal gave him a set of golf clubs, expensive and beautiful, his name stitched on the side of the stylish green bag. It was a thoughtful gift from all of them, clearly discussed and debated and selected with great care.

He managed gruff and appreciative as best he could.

Terry and some senior detectives bought him lunch at their favorite greasy spoon and wouldn't let him pay for his chicken potpie and iced tea.

His father's former secretary, who still handled his calendar, sent a stiffly formal birthday card and check, like Jim was sixteen and at boarding school, and wow, that brought up a lot of memories right there.

He deposited the check, then immediately wrote one twice the amount and stuck it in the mail to Liddy, Ben's wife. He told her to use it for a client who needed legal advice but didn't have the money up front.

Ed Kelly sent him a birthday card with a photograph of a beagle with a birthday hat on the front. Nothing sentimental or sweet inside, just a thanks and Ed's scrawl.

Jim tucked that into his jacket pocket.

The rest of the day was interspersed with a body found floating in the swimming pool of an abandoned house and Jim having to change his pants after a stabbing at a homeless shelter.

Nothing like dead bodies and bodily fluids to bring you back down to reality.

Then the phone call from Griffin Drake, and Jim was just…caught off guard. Jim was never off guard; he was permanently tense and anticipatory. But at the right moment (wrong moment?) the screenwriter called, offered to come take Jim for dinner, and Jim said yes, and that was how he was going to spend his forty-fifth birthday.

"Holy shit," he murmured as Terry gathered up his belongings and stood up to leave.

"Are you sure you won't come to dinner?" His partner clearly didn't believe the "going out with someone" story.

"I told you I have plans." Jim rearranged his desk and contemplated dusting his phone. He checked the clock and willed Terry out the door as quickly as possible.

"Real plans or fake plans?"

"Real plans." And hand to God, like the screenwriter had it all planned, Jim's cell phone buzzed at the same moment that Fredericks from second shift walked over and announced Jim had a visitor.

"They are real plans!" Terry said, looking smug and surprised at once.

"Go home. Please," Jim said a little desperately, answering his cell phone with a twist of his chair—like if he didn't look at Terry, he couldn't hear him.

Of course all he heard was Terry's briefcase thumping back on the desk and his partner settling in.

God.

"Jim Shea," Jim barked, and the pause on the other end told him it was, indeed, the screenwriter.

"Uh, Griffin Drake; I'm downstairs..."

"Right, I'll be down in a second." Jim used his free hand to quickly shut down his computer and collect his belongings, his face heated with embarrassment as both Terry and Fredericks watched. "Just wait for me at the desk."

"Right." The guy sounded a little nervous and surely regretting his trek to Seattle for dinner.

Jim promised himself he'd be on his best behavior all night if he could just get out of this building without an embarrassing scene.

He hung up and stood in one fast motion, grabbing his coat as he dodged Terry's amused look.

"Hey, I'll walk out with you," he said, and Jim glared.

"You're shameless."

"I'm *curious.*" Terry fell into step with him as they left the squad room.

"It's not a date. It's that screenwriter. We're just going to talk about the movie."

"On your birthday."

"He doesn't know that." Jim hit the Lobby button.

"So he just happened to call today, and you said yes because you actually had no real plans for your birthday."

Terry shook his head. "Really, Jim, we have to do something about your social life."

"I don't want a social life." The doors slid open and Jim tensed, glancing around for Griffin Drake—who was at the desk and looking exactly like a guy regretting making plans.

"Mr. Drake?" he called, striding away from Terry with a terse "night." He was sure he'd get the business tomorrow, but for now he just wanted to whisk this guy away from here.

"Detective Shea," Griffin Drake said, extending his hand warily. "I hope I'm not too early."

"No, no, perfect timing; let's go. I know a restaurant not too far from here," Jim rambled, ushering Mr. Drake toward the door.

"Night, Jim!" Terry called cheerfully as they headed for the door, just nearing their escape when he called out an additional "happy birthday!"

Jim winced. Busted.

They hit the cool night air, and Griffin turned to Jim, surprise on his face.

"It's your birthday? You should have told me, I would have never imposed myself—"

Jim cut him off, pulling his keys out of his pocket and hitting the button; his truck answered with a confirming *beep* as they got closer.

"Listen, I'll be straight with you. I didn't have any plans. You can go ahead and put that into your movie—workaholic detective does not have plans on his birthday," he said, opening the passenger-side door. He let his eyes linger on the younger man's face—and felt the unfortunate sympathy scalding. "That's a good character, right?"

"It's a cliché—I'm trying to get away from those," Griffin said, smiling brightly. "And technically, you have plans on your birthday. We're having dinner."

"Business…"

"Dude, I'm from Hollywood—I know how to combine business and pleasure perfectly."

Jim tried to pretend his blush was because of a sudden fever and not the feeling he was being charmed.

* * *

Jim made a pass at a diner he liked not too far from the station, but Griffin Drake vetoed that immediately. He started pressing buttons on his BlackBerry, muttering now and again, then gave Jim directions to a ritzier neighborhood, one he clearly didn't venture into very often.

"Here?"

"Pull up to the curb. Valet's waiting for you."

"Valet?"

Griffin looked at him under the dim lamp of the truck's overhead light. Jim could see the intelligence brewing in those dark eyes, and the furrow of his brow was easy to read. Jim was busted; this guy was a writer and that meant research, and that meant he knew Jim Shea had an excellent relationship with what fork to use at a restaurant like this one.

"We're probably not dressed for a place like this…" He made one last attempt, and Griffin smirked.

"Good thing you wear a suit to work and I'm about to flash a black American Express," he said drily, opening the door.

Jim clearly had lost both the first and second rounds of this evening.

Inside was dark and quiet, murmured conversation, and the clinking of glasses as waiters dodged around narrow tables, their all-black outfits making them seem like ghosts haunting the place, with platters of delicious-smelling food. The model-pretty girl at the front grabbed two menus and led them into the back, far from the narrow tables and into an intimate booth.

Jim tried not to physically react. Was this a date? This wasn't a date. Was this guy gay? Yeah, he was pretty sure the guy was gay, and he was gay, but this wasn't a date. Right? This couldn't be a date.

"Raul is your server this evening; he'll be right over," she said smoothly as Griffin slid into the booth and waited in the middle for Jim to move.

Aware he was a split second away from appearing a spectacle, Jim sat down.

"Thank you," Griffin said, all charm and floppy hair. He opened the menu, then looked up to see Jim hadn't moved. He tapped the cover with two fingers.

"Order anything. I'll expense it. This is a business dinner, after all."

There was something about the way he said it, something that poked Jim in the stomach and made him fidget.

"And it's your birthday."

"The waiters here don't sing, right? Or do a burning pile of ice cream with sparklers?" Jim resisted the urge to pull at his collar.

"I highly doubt it. But if you want me to find a place..."

"*No.*" Jim picked up his menu and squinted at the fancy script of the menu, desperately searching for the word "steak."

They sat in silence until Raul materialized at their table, hands clasped behind his back.

Before Jim could get anything out, Griffin ordered a bottle of expensive wine with their dinner—steak, but in French—and for starters, two beers.

Jim's jaw dropped a little.

Raul evaporated.

"Was that forward?" Griffin said suddenly, leaning forward. Jim could see the tiny tic under his left eye. "That was forward, wasn't it? I'm a little nervous."

"Why?"

"It isn't like me to be so...bold."

"Bold?"

"Have you ever noticed you talk predominantly in glares and one-word sentences?"

"I—sometimes." Jim tried to remember when his guard had fallen away completely and he was left sweating in the dark. Or maybe the tiny disc of a candle in the center of the table was producing way too much heat. "This whole movie thing is weird, okay? Having dinner with someone is weird too," he admitted reluctantly, drumming his fingers on the table.

"That's…"

"Pathetic?"

Griffin shrugged. "I spend many a night eating takeout with a laptop. My main social life is acting as an escort to my best friend at movie premieres, which sounds glamorous but really boils down to standing around and not getting enough to eat."

Jim raised one eyebrow. "Is this a contest?"

Griffin smirked, leaning his elbows on the table. "When's the last time you went grocery shopping…"

Jim opened his mouth.

"And bought more than just enough to get you through dinner and breakfast."

Jim's mouth snapped shut.

Griffin laughed.

By the time the beers arrived, Jim had ratcheted down from sweating and stressed to a near enjoyment of Griffin Drake.

And admitted to himself he wouldn't mind entirely if this turned into a date.

Chapter Seven

Griffin Drake was in trouble. Not the kind of trouble where you call for help—the kind of trouble where you make a sign of the cross and jump right in.

Detective Jim Shea, all six feet four, steel-jawed, and eyes the color of blue that he couldn't think of something creative for... God, what kind of writer was he? Right, the kind who was sitting across from a subject, a part of a larger puzzle, all but drooling in his crème brûlée.

They weren't talking much; Detective Shea clearly didn't do this very often. Griffin didn't either, but he was a natural talker, a social butterfly who dispelled every notion of the solitary, uncommunicative writer. He did like to drink, however, but he tried not to drink alone.

Which explained how the bottom of the wine bottle came up so soon.

"You want something else?" Griffin asked, well aware they hadn't touched the Kelly case or anything else beyond small talk about their respective cities and sports. He was already thinking of excuses to do this again—and to make this evening last a bit longer.

"Uh, I should probably have a pot of coffee." Jim Shea wiped his mouth with the linen napkin and rested it back on his lap. On the one hand, it was a natural movement; on the other, Griffin wanted to massage the tension out of his shoulders. "And not drive afterward." He looked regretfully at the empty wineglass and the almost empty second beer. "Not a smart move."

"I'd offer to drive, but you'd just have to pull me over," Griffin said, adding *and strip search me* in his head. "Let's have coffee, then…maybe take a walk? Clear our heads."

Jim nodded, looking around for the waiter. Griffin got an excellent view of that chiseled profile and movie-star jaw. If this guy weren't so stiff, he'd make a wickedly hot leading man.

Raul materialized, and Jim ordered a pot of coffee (black, of course). Griffin ran his hands through his hair—then discreetly rubbed off the sticky gel on the napkin in his lap.

Classy. He was a class act. And grateful this place was so damn dark.

"Thanks," Jim said suddenly, like a burst of sound he had been working up to. "For this dinner and, uh, not talking work. It's a nicer night than I imagined it being."

Griffin looked at the detective in surprise. He smiled, entirely pleased with himself.

"My pleasure. I planned on working you to death over cheap diner food, but this is much nicer," he teased gently, leaning his elbows on the table. "Seriously? I'm really glad I gave you a decent birthday dinner. You deserve it."

Jim's handsome face didn't reveal much agreement. He just looked embarrassed—like he wanted to disagree, but that would be rude.

"Come on, man, stop giving me that look. I used my writer Google fu, and frankly I'm stunned you didn't have a bunch of people throwing you a big party."

Jim's eyes dropped.

"Well, thanks. That's nice of you to say," Jim said stiffly. The coffee appeared before either of them could crawl under the table.

Griffin watched him pour his coffee, and his palms itched. The French wine, the night, the dark—it made him stupid ballsy.

"Why don't you believe that?"

"Huh?"

"Why don't you believe what I said? From what I can tell, you're well liked. Respected. Successful. You're not hurting for money or looks." He gnawed the inside of his mouth when that last word slipped out. "I'm not sure why I should feel bad for complimenting you."

Jim stirred his coffee aggressively. When he gestured with his spoon, tiny droplets of coffee flying across the table, Griffin reined in the urge to laugh.

"I don't like compliments."

Griffin let go of the reins.

"What? That's just… What does that mean? If I say - hey, Jim, nice shoes, that's a problem?"

"I don't trust them."

"Why?"

"I don't know. I just don't."

"You must be fun at parties."

"I don't go to parties."

Griffin rolled his eyes. "No parties, no compliments. Suddenly I'm understanding the lack of dating."

Jim's shoulders went up around his ears, and his eyes turned dark in the dim light. Griffin thought he might have to readjust himself under the table.

"Who said I don't date?"

"An educated guess."

"Do *you* date?"

"Occasionally." When Daisy made him.

Jim seemed stymied. He was clearly buying time by taking a sip of his coffee; Griffin enjoyed the tense silence.

Jim in control was hot. Jim slightly off-kilter was borderline illegal.

"Why don't you have a boyfriend?" Jim all but threw in an "aha" as punctuation.

"Don't want one," Griffin said breezily.

"Ever?"

"I want the right one."

"Lofty." Jim shook his head. "Unrealistic."

"To want to date the right person? How is that unrealistic? I'm sure you know people who are happy with each other."

"A few."

"Okay—so clearly they've found the right person. Why don't you think I can?"

"I don't mean *you* can't."

"You said…"

"I just meant it's hard to meet people, let alone the right person."

Griffin reached into his pocket and pulled out his BlackBerry. "Hang on, let me write down these pearls of wisdom. I'll use it for my next romantic comedy."

Jim made a face and Griffin laughed. Loudly. God, maybe he needed a cup of that coffee before he got loud drunk.

"You should try personal ads," Griffin teased. "Video dating."

"Shut up," Jim mumbled, stirring his coffee again.

"Maybe it's the bottle of wine talking here, Detective Shea, but I can't believe you walk down the street and don't get propositioned like twenty times a day. If I took you to a party back in my neck of the woods..."

"I'd spend the whole time busting people for possession," Jim finished.

"Hey...not the *whole* time."

"You don't..."

Griffin pondered this. "Are you going to narc me out for smoking a joint at Sundance last year?"

"I'll let it go this time," Jim said drily.

"Then I'm clean. I like my wine, I like my vodka tonics, I like the occasional beer with my red meat. I don't do drugs, I don't smoke, I don't jaywalk, and I only speed on the freeways where it is actually the law in Southern California."

"You sound like a great guy. Why aren't you being propositioned twenty times a day?"

It was clearly the closest thing to flirting Detective Shea was capable of.

Griffin was delighted.

"Well." Griffin pointed at his face. "Not exactly movie-star or male-model material, and where I live, that tends to help. Now, if I want to get laid, I just have to walk into a Starbucks and announce I'm a screenwriter. Then I have my pick of wannabes and head shots and sample scripts."

Jim frowned. "You're very... You look..." He huffed. "That's stupid."

"What's stupid? I didn't say I was hideous. Hell, I'd probably do fine if I moved somewhere less attractive."

"How are you going to find the right person if you think everyone is just trying to use you?"

Griffin had nothing. He wished for a cup of coffee. A spoon to stir it with.

"I think I liked it better when you were speaking in one-word sentences and glares," he said finally, cracking a smile. "So what's your excuse?"

"I…" Jim paused, appearing to actually be thinking of an honest answer. "I'm not good at it. I pick the wrong people, I say the wrong things. I'm better with…a few words, lots of glares."

"No dinners out, too many late nights, birthdays all alone." Griffin tapped his fingers on the dark shadow of the tablecloth. "Sucks."

"Maybe. Or it just is what it is."

"If I tell Daisy any of this, she's going to be working hard to fix you up." Daisy would be horrified by Jim's lack of romance. Horrified.

Jim looked panicked. "Please don't do that, or is this some sort of 'semi-husband and wife, we spill everything' deal?"

"Wow, good call."

"Why don't you marry *her*?"

"Well, for starters, she's already married. Also, her lady parts are of no interest to me."

"She's married?"

"Yeah." Griffin squirmed. Maybe he should shut up, ask for the check. Talking about his love life was slightly less dangerous than mouthing off about Daisy's. Not that Jim was going to excuse himself to call *Inside Edition*, but still. "For a long time, actually. It's complicated."

Griffin looked at Jim, who was clearly waiting for more.

"He owns the studio I work for. Bright Side." Griffin tried not to roll the words around in his mouth unpleasantly. Scaring Jim—and therefore Ed Kelly—off would be a disaster.

"So he's involved in Ed's movie?"

"No. That's a side project for Daisy and I."

Was that too quick? Too obviously a semi-lie?

"I don't know what that means."

"Like…a part-time job."

"Like a paper route."

"Yes, you're a paper route to me."

"No, Ed is a paper route to you. I'm Old Man Jenkins yelling for you to get off my lawn."

* * *

There was flirting, and then there was Jim cracking jokes. Or making jokelike statements. Griffin swallowed his tongue and searched around for the elusive Raul, who swooped in and saved the day by appearing and disappearing with Griffin's coveted Black Amex.

Jim watched him from across the table, wary and amused.

"I don't think I'm quite sober yet," he said, his voice slightly strained. "Think I'll take you up on that walk."

"Good idea." Griffin stared into the shadows, sidelong glances telling him that Jim was watching him.

"What time is your flight back?"

Griffin rolled his tongue around for a moment. "Don't have a ticket yet. I was playing it by ear."

Jim was quiet. "You got a hotel room?"

"Nope."

More silence.

Chapter Eight

Raul dropped off the snazzy black leather folder, and Griffin busied himself leaving a show-off tip and signing his name with a flourish.

"Let's go," Jim said, already standing up and brushing off his suit.

"Fresh air will do me good," Griffin mumbled.

They managed to find their way out of the dark maze, smelling fresh air and freedom and privacy. At least that's what Griffin was going by. He thought maybe Jim was just using his cop instincts.

No use in overplaying his hand—maybe the question about the hotel room was just Jim being polite.

The valet walked over as soon as they hit the cool, crisp night air. Griffin breathed deeply as Jim said they were walking around the block and would be right back.

He said this with a twenty-dollar bill. Then he started walking, and Griffin followed, moving his legs into an awkward jog to catch up.

"Don't leave without me," he said, and Jim slowed down slightly, looking at him with a touch of surprise.

"Sorry." He shook his head and laughed awkwardly. "I think I've forgotten how to walk leisurely."

"Wanna lean leisurely?" Griffin eyed a deeply shadowed doorway, a shop closed for the night.

"Not sure that'll clear my head."

Another pass at flirting. Griffin all but knocked him against the brick wall of the store as they reached it.

"Ah, fuck it," he said as they collided. Jim caught his weight, impacting the wall against his back as Griffin went in for a kiss.

Jim was surprised but alert enough, apparently, to catch Griffin and open his mouth at the same time.

Score.

Major score, because Jim's body felt exactly as good as Griffin imagined, rock hard under that sad gray suit. His mouth was equally good, or rather, great, and most importantly, willing.

They were just about the same height; Griffin's boots made up any difference, and it gave him enough leverage to push a bit harder. Full body against full body, the slowing down of that initial frantic kiss when you're fitting your mouths together for the first time.

Griffin went into leisurely mode, doing his damn best to make sure Detective Shea not only had a great birthday but also stayed on board their little project.

He was the ultimate unselfish guy—with a fistful of Jim's lapels and his tongue doing an exploration of the detective's oral cavity. The leg slide, the imposition of his thigh between legs of steel…all the moves were working, and Jim didn't seem to want to flip him over and punch his lights out.

It was all really good, even when Jim tipped his head to one side to suck in a lungful of air.

Griffin half tensed, waiting for the rejection, but nothing came except Jim's hands on his face, tilting him to the perfect angle before the kissing started up again.

Heaven.

Griffin pushed in a little more until they were flush against each other, dueling belt buckles and burgeoning erections, Jim's hands sliding down to Griffin's ass with an impossible-to-ignore signal.

Not to be outdone, Griffin used whatever muscles he'd worked up in the gym and yanked Jim's hips forward—and duplicated his move.

Jim came up for breath again and gave him an interesting look.

Quizzical. Slightly worried. Really turned on. Griffin squeezed Jim's ass a little tighter, brushing his fingers against the seam of those equally sad gray pants.

Jim moaned under his breath, and Griffin wished for a genie to grant him three wishes—a bed, a condom, and a bottle of Astroglide.

"Let's get out of here—you're sober, right? Because I'm really, really sober right now," Griffin babbled, not bothering to wait for an answer. He ducked his head and went for the spot of skin just above Jim's collar.

"Uh, you're going to have to let me go," Jim pointed out weakly, putting his hands on Griffin's shoulders and giving him a shove.

They were maybe a foot apart, both breathing heavily. Griffin tried to get his equilibrium back, a vain attempt punctuated by trying to cover his enormous erection with the hem of his jacket and smoothing his hair out of his eyes.

Stupid gel. Twenty-four bucks for a tube of that crap, and it didn't survive making out with an incredibly hot guy. He was going to write a letter to…someone.

"Okay, let's go. Not giving you a chance to change your mind."

Jim straightened his suit with shaky hands. "What makes you think I'll change my mind?"

Griffin shrugged. The first thing that came to his lips was so very *un*bold; the idea that this ridiculously hot guy would want to sleep with him was straight out of bizarre world.

"I thought this wasn't your thing."

"What? Sex? Good news, I'm not a virgin." Jim started walking back toward the restaurant, hands dug into his pockets.

"Dating, with a sex chaser." Griffin caught up with another swift jog. This guy was great for his cardio.

"Rare, but it happens."

"I feel honored."

"Or maybe I'm desperate." Jim gave him a triumphant smirk, but Griffin just laughed and kicked his walk up a few more leg movements per second.

"Then lucky me, to catch Detective Jim Shea on an off night."

They reached the valet in record time; Jim flipped the guy two more twenties, and Griffin whistled under his breath.

The guy respected the bribe and pretended not to notice their rumpled state or their hurry to get into the truck and get the hell out of Dodge.

* * *

"How far do you live from here?" Griffin asked, buckling himself in as Jim pulled onto the quiet street.

"Fifteen minutes." Jim drove slowly, with extra pauses at the stop signs. "Maybe twenty."

"My ego is wounded—why aren't you in a hurry?"

"Because I'm a cop who had a few with dinner, and if I got stopped, my career is fucked." Jim gave him a withering, tough-guy look that Griffin found vaguely hot.

"Got it." Griffin did a "lock the lips and throw away the key" motion, which earned him an equally hot eye roll.

They drove in silence, listening to the low murmur of an all-news radio station and the occasional horn honk of someone who didn't appreciate Jim's overly cautious style of driving.

When Griffin saw the little market on the corner, a thought rose up that both embarrassed and entertained him.

"Can we stop?" He pointed out the market. Jim looked surprised.

"Okay, but, uh, if you need anything, I probably have it."

God, was he blushing?

"I'm positive you don't have what I'm going to pick up."

"Now I'm scared…"

But Jim pulled over anyway, and Griffin jumped out of the truck.

* * *

Five minutes later he was back with a small bag, the contents of which he refused to show Jim. This might backfire, but…but it felt right in a strange way. He was going with his gut at the moment and praying for the best.

"I'm only around the block," Jim said.

"Perfect timing, then."

Jim eased the giant pickup down a side street and into a wide parking spot. When the truck was shut off, the lights out, Griffin leaned over the cab and slid his hand behind Jim's neck.

"You wanna neck in the truck?" Jim asked lightly—questioning yet not resisting at all.

"Nah, just want to make sure you're still into this."

Jim didn't answer, he just closed his eyes and opened his mouth, and Griffin thought maybe making out in the cab was a great idea.

It didn't get that far; a few pumps of mutual tongues, some teeth on Jim's bottom lip, and he pulled away with a mumble about getting upstairs.

Griffin followed with his backpack and his grocery bag and his renewed hard-on and eyes glued to Jim's back. They entered the corner building, which resembled a factory, but once inside, Griffin could see the amazing interiors.

"Art deco? Wow. You'd never guess from outside," he murmured, taking in the sharp artwork and mirrors. The elevator opened with a twist of Jim's key.

"It's like a pleasant surprise every time I come home."

That admission caught Griffin's attention and he smiled, pleased that Jim had shared it.

"How long have you been here?"

"Since I got out of the army." They stepped into the elevator, and Jim pressed the top number—eleven. "Almost fifteen years. Started as a renter, lived through the renovations, bought it about ten years ago."

The doors opened smoothly, and Jim gestured Griffin into the darkened loft. "Home sweet home."

Griffin stepped out.

There was an echo.

"Should I be nervous?" Griffin asked as the light switched on. Okay, a relief—no torture chamber, just very little furniture and very high ceilings.

"Only if you fear cleanliness." Jim stripped off his jacket and moved into the small kitchen area to the left.

Chapter Nine

Cleanliness was an understatement; Griffin wouldn't have been surprised if you could actually perform surgery on the polished wood floor or clutter-free counter space.

He pulled off his coat and hung it neatly on the coatrack, left his bag on the floor out of the way. The cavernous space felt cool and put a kibosh on Griffin's moves for the moment. He was curious to know more of Detective Jim Shea, who lived in a sterile loft decorated by IKEA.

Jim poured them drinks; Griffin could hear the ice clinking into glasses. He walked through the tidy living room, eyes on the lookout for pictures or trophies, mementos. Those Officer of the Year plaques, maybe. Maybe a magazine or book or selection of questionable DVDs about hot male nurses.

But nothing, not a single thing. If this were a set, it wouldn't tell anything about the person who lived here. Except that he managed to keep the place dusted at a professional level.

"Here—it's just seltzer," Jim said, coming up behind him. "I'm outta beer—haven't been to the grocery store in a while," he said drily.

Griffin took the glass without comment. He wanted to ask about the lack of personalization, but really, the answer had already manifested itself in the way Jim nervously suffered through this date and Griffin's haphazard seduction.

"No problem, I think I'm buzzed enough," he said finally, stepping into Jim's personal space with a swagger. "How are you feeling?"

Jim laughed. "Weird."

"Decidedly unflattering."

Jim shook his head, opened his mouth, then closed it—instead of saying anything more, he leaned forward to lay a warm kiss on Griffin's mouth.

Not a chewing, rough kiss of intent; more of a thank-you or a good-night or a welcome-home sort of kiss, one that Griffin didn't associate with a one-night stand. It weirded him out for a moment, inciting his lizard brain to perhaps bolt out of the loft in sheer terror.

Except he didn't really want to do that. He wanted to stay as he returned the gentle kiss.

Because now Griffin had a good handle on at least one of Jim Shea's secrets—he really was a romantic.

"I think I need a tour, starting with the bedroom," Griffin said, sliding a hand around to Jim's back.

"Subtle."

"Not going for subtle." Griffin tried to offset the seriousness of his voice with a smile, and Jim relaxed a little under his hand.

Jim led him to the wide, open staircase near the double glass doors filling most of the back wall. Beyond most likely lay a kick-ass view of Seattle at night, but Griffin was more concerned with Jim, the romantic, shy guy who lived in a loft with hardly any furniture.

The stairs didn't take long, though Griffin had a hard time keeping his hands to himself. At the top, he peered over and spotted the exact bed he would have asked that genie for.

The huge, four-poster modern monstrosity took up nearly all the open loft space. White sheets, white comforter, piles of thick white pillows stacked at the top. All that was missing were the chocolates on the pillow.

"That's your bed? Griffin stepped past Jim, still holding on to him.

Jim laid his half-empty glass on the matching dresser to the side.

"Like it?" There was a distinct note of pride in his voice.

"You may never get me out of here," Griffin mumbled under his breath, following suit with his own full glass. "Where were we? Oh, right…"

He didn't let Jim wander too far; he rubbed flat palms over Jim's chest and stomach to reacquaint himself with that fine body. He wanted to move to the part where Jim was naked, but the anticipation was enough for now.

"Let's lie down," he murmured, hands moving to unbutton the other man's shirt. "More comfortable that way." He loosened Jim's shirt and reached for his belt as Jim slowly set him on fire with a sultry look. First the buttons, then the belt, then the awkward and sexy shimmy out of his pants. Griffin ran his tongue over his lips, then mimicked the move on Jim's mouth until they both swayed.

Griffin gave Jim a tiny push toward the bed, that swagger back again. The straining erection tenting those Boy Scout tighty whities told him everything he wanted—but Jim's eyes explained what he needed. It made him feel like a god to know that so clearly, without words being said.

"No boots on the bed," Jim said, cheeky and breathless. And ridiculously hot. Griffin felt his retinas burning as his eyes raked over Jim's muscled body.

"You're going to vacuum when I fall asleep, aren't you?"

"No. Maybe," Jim admitted, lying back on the bed. "I might dust too."

"Well, then I'm going to have to work hard to make sure you can't move." Griffin toed off his boots and pushed them to the side, following with his socks and shirt. Now in an undershirt and jeans, he walked slowly to stand next to the bed.

If he thought too much, he would be overwhelmed by how this man made him feel. Jim Shea was so far out of his league that he thought this might be Opposite Day. Because in the real world, men who looked like Jim got one look at his slightly geeky exterior and pegged Griffin for a good-time bottom who would understand why they never called after that night.

Jim Shea didn't look at him that way. His blue eyes were needy and hopeful and apprehensive, and Griffin soaked it up. He couldn't keep Jim waiting another second; he pressed his hands on the firm mattress, palms flat on either side of

Jim's massive shoulders. Jim didn't move, he just sort of…exhaled…and Griffin's slow route got detoured.

He swung one leg over Jim's hips and knelt over him.

Jim still didn't move, though the energy and anticipation leaped up into Griffin's skin. He leaned down, licking his lips as their eyes held until the last second—and then that slow, sexy kissing ignited once again.

Griffin loved to kiss, loved that hungry push of tongues and teasing chase. He loved the taste of a man—in this case, Jim was steak and coffee with a piece-of-gum chaser, exactly the way Mr. Tough Guy should taste.

All that power and strength stayed coiled, though; Griffin knew that Jim could toss him across the room if he wanted, but clearly all he was angling for right now was Griffin pressing him down on the bed.

Jim's hands came up, strong but tentative, and four seconds later Griffin was engulfed by his white T-shirt—then that was gone. The cool air made him shiver, but Jim took care of that too, ghosting his fingers over Griffin's bare skin.

Will not flinch, not ticklish right at this really perfect moment, he thought, moving his mouth off and on Jim's to catch his breath. "Feels good," he murmured, gently reassuring Jim as his eyes drifted closed. Those callused fingers counted his ribs, diagrammed his spine, and drifted around to rub over Griffin's nipples.

"Ahhh, amazingly good." Griffin exhaled, dropping his ass down to sit on Jim's upper thighs as his hand moved to Jim's fly. He needed relief; Jim seemed to think so too as their fingers joined together to unbutton and unzip the fly all the way down. This brought those overabused erections against each other again through dampening cotton, and both men moaned.

And then Griffin moaned louder, because damn, that little concert sounded hot.

"We should, uh… How about me without my pants?" Griffin talked under his breath, scrabbling at the waistband of his jeans. Of course it wasn't going to work unless he stood up—a quick look revealed the ceiling fan pretty high up, and he unfolded off Jim to stand and unbutton his jeans.

And looked down to see himself straddled over Jim—who was laughing.

"Something funny?"

"No." Jim kept smiling, though.

Griffin tried to breathe and kick off the jeans without falling off the bed. Because he was damned if this evening was going to end with him in an emergency room.

Now sans jeans, Griffin put his hands on his hips and shot Jim his best sexy-pirate look. Jim tucked his hands behind his head and shot a sexy look up of his own.

It was all mind-blowingly perfect, like he'd written this man and date and moment himself. And now, because it was real life and not a movie set, Griffin was starting to catch a cool breeze. He dropped back down to his knees, once again straddling Jim's marble-sculpted body.

"You wanna… I need…" Griffin fumbled for a moment, sucked dry of proper word usage as Jim surged up against him. They were face-to-face, and Jim didn't look so amused anymore. He looked starving.

"Left nightstand, top drawer," he answered, quick and quiet. Griffin nodded, then leaned forward for a kiss, twining his hands together at the back of Jim's neck, rubbed his palms against the tense cords of the other man's skin.

He lost himself again in Jim and the kiss, open mouths and quick, darting tongues.

"Just so you know, I'm a product of the eighties and a latex king. Very clean," Griffin managed between kisses. Jim nodded and pulled Griffin down on top of him, pushed his knees up so Griffin's weight was heavy on his chest.

It was the perfect position for kissing, the ideal angle for rubbing dick against dick, their respective pairs of underwear both a hindrance and a help to keep from popping off too soon; Griffin supposed it might be where he'd like to live forever.

The urge to fuck was still there—very strong, very much so—but Griffin felt contentment spreading through his bones, thick and hot. Jim didn't seem in a hurry either, hands tangling through Griffin's hair and down his back.

Another deep stroke of his tongue and Jim bucked upward; Griffin felt a fire pumping up in his blood and pressed his palms against Jim's shoulders.

He held him down and kissed him and tasted the breathless moans, and the urge to fuck roared back.

He attacked Jim's granite jawline and down his neck, running his teeth over the sharp pulse. Vampiric urges swelled up as he tested the strength of his teeth against Jim's skin until he felt the...give...until he felt that he could burst through and taste Jim and yeah, taste him—he wanted to taste him.

"Put your legs down," Griffin ground out, shimmying down until he could kneel between Jim's spread-open knees, looking up at that vast landscape of man—desperate, hot, wanting man whose expectation made Griffin smile wickedly.

"Hold on," he said as he grabbed the waistband of Jim's underwear and pulled down.

Chapter Ten

Jim grabbed handfuls of the cool comforter beneath him as Griffin pulled his underwear off. They went sailing across the room, and Jim arched his back, unable to even pretend this wasn't exactly what he wanted. Embarrassment made him turn his head to one side, to find a hiding space in the folds of the pillow behind his head.

"Oh no, no hiding," Griffin said, his hands dragging down the insides of Jim's thighs and pushing his knees apart again. "Come on, just enjoy yourself. Happy birthday and all that junk."

There was a cajoling humor to Griffin's voice that he could neither ignore nor resist. Jim blinked and looked up at the other man, at the pleased smile and amused eyes, and nodded.

He'd let it happen. He'd have a good time. He'd let this very likable young man give him what he wanted and not feel guilty or weird. Happy goddamn birthday to him.

His body relaxed the slightest bit, and Griffin apparently took this as a sign to go; he leaned down to rub a wet kiss on the lower part of his abdomen.

Jim exhaled.

"There you go," Griffin muttered, sweeping to the side and focusing his kisses on the inside of Jim's left thigh. His dick throbbed in anticipation, but he didn't get pushy, didn't get demanding. He let himself take a second to enjoy someone enjoying *his* body.

The left knee got some attention, then the right, then up to the crease where leg met torso. Every muscle Jim worked so diligently in the gym received some of Griffin's warm mouth, mapping his body like there was a quiz later and he was determined to get an A.

Jim babbled appreciatively under his breath as he tried not to twist with need under Griffin's ministrations. Foreplay? Did he remember foreplay? Did he remember this much? The ceiling drew his attention up as Jim tried to zone out on the unmoving blades of the fan.

"Goodfuckinghell" flew out of his mouth suddenly as all his attention was brought back to the here and now as Griffin surprise deep throated him in one admirable move.

Jim's eyes went down, locked into the very pleased visage of Griffin Drake, who swallowed him down until his eyes rolled back in his head.

"Um." Jim wheezed, forcing his hips to stay on the bed. It didn't last long as Griffin pulled back slightly, just enough to raise himself up and push Jim's legs open wider. He was exposed, open and shaking with eagerness; shame would have sprung further into his mind, but Griffin didn't give him the time.

He rubbed his hands against the backs of Jim's thighs, his head bobbing up and down as he sucked his dick with a lazy effort that nonetheless had Jim biting his bottom lip.

Jim wanted to tell him to hurry, but all that happened when he opened his mouth was a string of shaky moans with a few curse words thrown in.

He looked down again, and Griffin managed to grin around his mouthful of Jim's erection. After a second he pulled off, the popping sound loud and obscene enough to echo across the loft.

Griffin didn't let go of Jim's thighs, and that wicked look didn't appear to be going anywhere either.

"How anal are you exactly?" he asked, all smirk and dimples—how did Jim miss the dimples?

"Uh." Jim moaned—really, he was going to protest, because that was disgusting and they hardly knew each other and who the ever-loving hell was he kidding with this line of bullshit dancing between his ears?

"I knew it," Griffin muttered; he turned his head just enough to nip at the inside of Jim's knee.

Then he went down lower, and Jim's breath hiccupped.

His arms went straight out, flexing his shoulders as he grabbed hold of the comforter. If anyone hovered above him, they'd have thought that Jim was in pain, that he was about to be tortured.

But the first tentative flick of Griffin's tongue against his ass was anything but torture.

Christ, did he remember the last time he let anyone get this close? He made a promise to blame the wine and the beer and the day when morning came.

* * *

Griffin was a tease. He gave Jim a few licks, just enough to leave him shaking and babbling, then hummed his way back up, still holding Jim in that vulnerable, open position.

"What are you...?"

"Shut up," Griffin said, still smirking but now a little more out of breath. A little more needy.

"Need a hand?" Jim tried for cheeky but just sounded desperate.

"Need a condom and about four gallons of lube," Griffin mumbled, his mouth roaming randomly over Jim's dick and stomach and inner thighs.

"Let go of me..."

"No, not yet. Need that eventually. Really need to fuck you, but for now..." And then he was gone, back to flick and circle and preview what was (hopefully) coming very, very soon. Before Jim came quickly and had to apologize and oh— everything flew sideways out of his head as Griffin stopped playing and pushed the tip of his tongue into Jim's body.

"Oh God." Jim moaned, letting go entirely. It had been so long since he'd let anyone fuck him that this prelude to the act was his undoing. He knew what was going to happen, exactly what he was going to let this guy do, and while a fleeting part of him panicked, the rest of him—locked up for so long—felt relief and burning anticipation.

Griffin Drake, of course, had no idea about any of this; he was tongue fucking Jim, his hands gripping his thighs, and no doubt trying to remember where Jim said the condom and lube was.

"Please." The word finally leaked from Jim's mouth.

Griffin heard him—maybe he was just as anxious to move on as Jim. The last press of his tongue was a slow push in and quick twist out. Jim grasped the bottom of his dick in a desperate attempt not to come. Mumbling something about "hot," Griffin gently let Jim's legs down and swarmed over him with more of those openmouthed kisses. His dick, his hand, his stomach, up to Jim's mouth.

There was a moment's pause, a request for permission, and Jim nodded, arching his neck up and opening his mouth for a kiss.

* * *

"Come on, roll over," Griffin murmured when he came up for air. Jim liked the husky growl of his voice and the way his messed-up hair now fell over his forehead. He looked younger in the dim light—but there was nothing immature about the way he was moving his hands over Jim's body. He knew what he wanted—what they both wanted.

"Top drawer," he said as a reminder, sitting up for one last kiss before he rolled out from under Griffin's body and onto his stomach.

His ego got a nice stroke from the moan that followed his motion.

Griffin mumbled to himself as he leaned over Jim's body and yanked the drawer open. Jim folded his arms and laid his face down in the gap, just enough air to breathe, but plenty of cool pillow to tune down the hot flush of his cheeks.

The pressure of mattress against his dick? Very helpful.

"What? No flavored lube? No neon-colored condoms? Stunned, Jim, stunned," Griffin said, making noises and then dropping the unflavored lube and regular condom-colored condoms on the small of Jim's back.

"Shut up." Jim laughed. That felt as good as the mattress. Almost as good as the sound of a tearing condom packet and Griffin's mutterings. Or the warm hand that Griffin laid against the space between Jim's shoulder blades, as if letting him know he hadn't forgotten him.

Best birthday ever, Jim thought. Better than twenty-one and Vegas.

* * *

Griffin didn't rush the next bit, no matter how much Jim threatened or begged.

He pushed Jim onto his knees, kissing and stroking his body, talking so quietly that Jim only heard a comforting hum into his ears.

Just a drop too much lube. Two fingers. A brush of tongue and really—Jim's cursing wound out of control at that point. He'd wanted it since Griffin had ambushed him with a kiss and touched him when they left the restaurant. But now the thought of *this* moment in his life exploded into his bloodstream. He wanted it now, and he couldn't wait.

"Gimme a sec, okay?" Griffin was breathing heavily now, words slurred with lust. He pushed Jim down a little, leveraged his legs farther apart. Jim felt the other man's breath midway down his back. He moved higher and higher until Griffin fit snuggly against him, curling over his body, one hand fumbling between them.

"Can't wait," Jim moaned and pushed back, catching the blunted head of Griffin's dick as he did.

"Ohfuckinggod." Griffin didn't waste another second, pressing into Jim with a blessed sigh of relief.

Jim put his head down against the pillow; he bit down on the soft fabric as Griffin pushed and rocked and worked his cock into Jim's body. There was a hellacious pause as Griffin squeezed his fingers tight into his hips—sparks of pain and pleasure mixed with Jim's blessed sense of fullness.

Nothing was said, no sounds emitted by either one of them. The squeak of the bed seemed ridiculously loud as Griffin leaned back, then forward.

One stroke, and Jim shook with the sheer pleasure of it. He tensed every muscle in his body so he could feel everything Griffin gave. Two strokes. Three. Griffin thrusting against him, damp with sweat and digging his fingers deeper and deeper into Jim's flesh.

Four strokes. Five. Jim started to lose count, began to lose control over his muscles. Griffin seemed to be growing stronger and rougher as Jim lost his ability to stay upright.

Six. Ten? Jim's arms gave out, and he was just held up by his knees now and Griffin's firm grip on his body, inside and out.

Lost now, Jim moaned into the pillow, fingers digging into the material until darts of pain began to form as they cramped. The bed shrieked and panted under Griffin's forceful strokes, and Jim begged along, completely caught in the rhythm.

There was almost no warning when Jim came, no shout or even an attempt at words. Griffin caught him with a sharp downward stroke and hit something deep inside him, more than a bit of anatomy. It pulled the trigger, and he let it go, catching his cock on the edge of the rucked-up sheets as he came.

Griffin followed him down as his knees slid open, and he was flat on the bed, still absorbing the impact of Griffin's sharp thrusts. Hands laid on his shoulders, the strength of being held down setting Jim's body aflame again. Griffin sped up, muttering and moaning as he rushed to his own completion.

He fell down onto Jim's back.

"Hmmmph," he murmured against Jim's shoulder.

"Huh?" His brain didn't seem to have engaged just yet.

"Happy fucking birthday." Griffin laughed, rubbing his forehead against the sweaty skin on the back of Jim's neck.

"You're not getting a thank-you note."

"Rude."

Jim settled into the bed. He thought about the stickiness on the sheets and on his body. He thought about the clothes scattered around. He was very much aware of Griffin sprawled over him, only moving enough to pull out and take care of the condom.

"Garbage?"

"Next to the nightstand."

Griffin didn't get up. Jim heard the tossed condom hit the empty garbage can, followed by a few clicks of plastic. The nightstand drawer opened and closed…and Jim realized that Griffin was cleaning up.

"Stop—I'll do that later," Jim said, finally moving his head from the pillow and turning to the other man.

"Yeah, I know. When you get the vacuum out." Griffin lay on his side, running his hand over Jim's back. His smile was dorky, his hair now completely rumpled and sideways on his head. He squinted, then rubbed at his eyes carefully.

"Contacts bugging you?"

"Yeah. I'm gonna run down to the bathroom. You need something?"

"No, I got it." Jim still didn't move, however. That blissful, fucked-out feeling gave him no immediacy at all.

"No, you lie here. I'll be right back." Griffin rolled off the bed and fumbled for a second for his jeans, throwing them over his shoulder as he jogged down the stairs. He whistled, and Jim could see he was clearly pleased with himself.

His face got warm as he smiled into the pillow.

Chapter Eleven

"You need help down there?" Jim called, listening carefully to get a hint of what Griffin was doing. Definitely in the kitchen and rooting around. Well, it wasn't like he was going to find much beyond some crackers, protein bars, and leftover pad thai.

The trip to the bathroom had produced Griffin in jeans, his glasses, and bearing a warm, wet washcloth. He'd tidied their clothes up as Jim cleaned up, then stripped off the top coverlet and sheet, quickly replacing them with "military efficiency," as Griffin named it. Then he'd snapped his fingers and declared he had another surprise.

"Nope. And no peeking!"

"Not peeking! Mostly because if I lean over the railing, I might end up on my head. Emergency room isn't how I want to spend the rest of the night."

From down below, Griffin cackled.

"Okay, coming up. Close your eyes."

"This isn't a weird food kinky thing, because…you know, crumbs and stuff on the bed…" Jim shivered at the thought.

Griffin didn't say anything, but Jim could hear him coming up the stairs. Then he saw the little light.

A candle, coming up the stairs, and Jim didn't quite understand until he heard the off-key rendition of "Happy Birthday."

He sat up, tenting the sheet under his knees, trying to form an expression and a response.

He was…touched. Embarrassed. Overwhelmed.

His face formed into a smile as he watched Griffin approach with two Hostess cupcakes on a plate, a small emergency tea light candle on each.

"Make a wish," Griffin said shyly, sitting on the bed and offering the plate to Jim.

Jim took a deep breath and thought—I really can't think of anything at the moment except maybe for this moment to last—and blew the two little candles out.

"I hope this is okay…" Griffin's voice sounded pleased, but the note of uncertainty was something Jim understood quite well. It was a gesture, a big one. He wanted it to go over well.

"Thank you," Jim broke in, reaching to run his hand over Griffin's bare arm. "This might be the nicest thing anyone's done for me in a few dozen years."

That pleased Griffin immensely. He waved the cupcakes under Jim's nose, that look of goofy swagger reappearing.

"Eat your cupcakes."

"Don't you get one?"

"Nah, I'm just gonna watch and be all pleased with myself, and then I'm going to lick the chocolate off your mouth."

Jim blinked; his hand stopped midway to the chocolate treat.

"I'm a very neat eater." He smirked, taking the cupcake in hand. Bits of chocolate on his white sheets gave him a twitch normally, but he might just make the exception tonight.

"Then maybe I'll bounce on the bed to create smears." Griffin stripped out of his unbuttoned jeans and got back into bed—with an extra bit of effort to try and dislodge the cupcake.

"Smears is not a sexy word."

"Neither is crumbs, but admit it—the licking of the chocolate line, that was hot."

"Mmmph." Jim bit the cupcake in half, the taste of artificial sugar exploding on his tongue. Heaven. And a good call. Most people would take a look at him and think all soy and no play, but nothing beat a chocolate treat made in a chemical plant sometimes.

He gave Griffin a sideways look and offered him a bite as he chewed.

"Okay, maybe just a taste." Griffin smiled, leaning in to lick the bits of chocolate crumbs off Jim's fingers before biting into the moist cake.

Jim smirked as Griffin chewed with a blissful smile of his own. "Okay, the French food was nice, but damn if these cupcakes aren't good."

"Little did you know, I'm a cheap date." Jim broke the second cupcake in half and handed the other piece to Griffin, who didn't even protest.

"Eh, next time I'll let you take me to that diner."

Jim pondered the "next time" as he ate, careful not to spill any crumbs—then realized that Griffin was watching him out of the corner of his eye. "What?"

"What what?"

Jim put the plate on the nightstand and licked the chocolate off his fingers. Griffin was sitting there, still with the cupcake in his hands. "Why are you sitting there like that? Eat the cupcake before I reconsider my generous sharing and take it back."

Griffin put the chocolate cake in his mouth, throwing Jim looks now and again.

"What?"

Griffin swallowed. "Just wanna make sure it's cool if I stay here tonight."

Jim snorted. "No. Get your shit and get out." He snapped the new sheet over them and contemplated another blanket.

Griffin didn't lie back right away, even as Jim restacked the pillows and lay down.

"That was a joke."

"I know." Griffin sounded a little defensive, but he lay down anyway, rubbing his hands over his hair.

"I'm having a good time. Wasn't what I expected at all, but it's…fun."

"You sound surprised."

"I thought we established I don't know how to have fun. Or date," Jim said drily.

"Oh, right." There was a pause. "So this is a date."

"Well, technically. Unless all your business dinners end this way." Jim turned his head to give Griffin a stern look. "Do they?"

"God, no." That finally elicited a laugh from Griffin.

"All right, then." Jim folded his arms behind his head and contemplated another blanket for a second time. "So we had a date. And it, uh…went well, I think."

"I think so." Griffin coughed theatrically.

"Are you ready to sleep?"

"You're the one with the actual job that requires an alarm clock. I'm gonna sleep until you kick my ass out. This bed is amazing."

Jim threw back the sheet and slid out of bed, his muscles echoing that yes, this was a date, and it was a good one. He walked to the closet to grab the second comforter and heard a wolf whistle. And snickering.

"Shut up. Just for that, I'm waking your ass up at five a.m."

Jim threw the comforter over Griffin, then climbed back into bed.

"Five? That's like—six hours from now." Griffin sounded horrified. "That's not enough sleep."

"I have to be in by eight," Jim said, kicking the sheets around until they were the way he liked them—and realized that he hadn't shared a bed since Matt in New York.

"God, real jobs are horrifyingly early."

Jim considered telling him that usually he slept for two hours, went to the gym, and was at his desk by six a.m., but he didn't.

"Yeah, what can I tell you? But, uh…you don't have to get up that early. You can sleep, hang out. Whatever."

Jim rolled over to face Griffin, who was still half sitting up, a surprised expression on his face.

"Wow—thanks. I was joking before…"

"Well, I'm not joking now. Just sleep in, do whatever you want. We can, uh…have lunch if you're still around."

It's just polite. Payback for the dinner. At least that's what Jim attempted to tell himself.

"Okay, sure. Thanks." Griffin finally settled down under the covers, watching Jim as he pulled the covers up to his neck. "So you know, this is like that weird moment when you drop someone off at the end of the night and aren't sure if you should kiss them…"

"We're a little bit past that point."

"Yeah, clearly. I haven't ever dropped anyone off at their front door naked."

"Good to know, good to know."

They were close enough to kiss, and Jim thought that might be a nice idea actually. He thought about Griffin's move on the street after dinner and smiled, rolling closer as he snaked his arm around Griffin under the covers, pulling their bodies flush.

"I had a very nice evening; thank you so much for dinner," Jim said politely.

Griffin snickered. "You're so welcome, Jim. I hope I can call on you again."

Jim lifted his head and angled his mouth against Griffin's.

* * *

Eventually Griffin drifted off, facedown on the pillow and snoring lightly. Jim listened to the sounds, felt the warmth of another person beside him, and watched the lazy circles of the ceiling fan move shadows over the walls.

When the day started, he'd dreaded the outcome. He had no expectations, let alone expectations of going to sleep next to someone like Griffin.

He could still taste the kisses on his lips, the chocolate...

He drifted off before he could remember that he never fell asleep this early or this easily.

* * *

When the alarm beeped at seven, Jim's eyes shot open, his heart racing. He sat up and glanced at the red numbers, wondering for a moment if it was a dream. He didn't remember setting it for so late; he was usually at his desk already...

"Sorry," a voice mumbled sleepily next to him. "Got up to pee around four and realized you hadn't set it, so...hope seven is okay."

Griffin. Jim took a deep breath and nodded, clearing his throat. "No, thanks. I completely forgot."

"Yeah, you were out." Griffin snuffled at the pillow, then smiled up myopically in Jim's direction. "You want me to make coffee or something?"

"No, no, go back to sleep. I'm gonna grab a shower and get out of here. I'll call you later." Jim's heart still thudded in his chest as he swung his legs over the side of the bed.

"Cool." Griffin rolled back over, taking the bulk of the comforter with him.

Jim stumbled downstairs and straight to the shower.

* * *

There was some vague soul-searching as Jim looked up at the showerhead, mostly involving the ease of this "date." Jim presumed that was because of Griffin and his easygoing nature and charm. Hell, if all the guys he met were like Griffin, he'd be okay with the idea of dinner and sex and waking up and second dates.

All guys, however, were not like Griffin, or at least Jim was bad at meeting them.

Eventually the water turned cool and Jim hustled out. He was starting to actually consider the possibility of being "late"—and that never happened.

Clicking into high gear, Jim skipped shaving, brushed his teeth, and raced back upstairs to grab a suit. He was halfway down the stairs when he realized he smelled coffee.

Griffin was standing at the counter, stirring a mug of coffee. A second sat on the edge of the counter, waiting.

"Milk or sugar?" Griffin called, yawning widely.

"Black." Jim tied his tie, trying to be casual about a naked, hair-askew Griffin leaning against the countertop.

"Of course." Griffin gathered up the mug and put the spoon in the sink.

Jim grabbed his keys as he slid on his shoes. "I'll, uh… There are extra keys here by the door and the elevator one…that's on the red cord."

"'Kay." With another huge yawn, Griffin walked over and rubbed his forehead. "Gonna sleep a few more hours; then I'll give you a call."

"Great." There was a pause, and Jim felt the urge to say something else or…

Griffin, of course, reacted before he could formulate something; he leaned in and kissed Jim hot and dirty, a coffee-flavored delving of his oral cavity that completely belied the sleepy expression on his face.

"Later." Griffin took a step back and shuffled off, nude and clutching the coffee mug.

Eventually Jim clicked his jaw shut, took his own mug, and headed into the elevator.

Chapter Twelve

Terry didn't just toss an onion bagel on Jim's desk with an easy lie as soon as he walked in—he threw the bagel, then rolled his chair around to sit next to Jim, grande tea in hand and an expectant smile on his face.

"So…"

"Good morning, Terry. How was your evening?" Jim asked, professional and innocent as a babe as he peeled the wrapper off the bagel. "By the way, could you ask them to make a mistake with a raisin-walnut tomorrow? Lightly toasted with butter."

Terry waved his cup. "Yeah, sure—my evening was lovely, change of bagel…now talk."

"About what?" Jim took a bite of his bagel.

"You and the screenwriter."

"We had dinner."

"And?"

"And what?"

Terry smirked. "You have a mark on your neck."

"Shaving."

"You bit yourself shaving?"

"Okay, you got me. The screenwriter is a vampire. Now go to your own desk and call Mimi so she can call me and I can get my day started."

Laughing, Terry took a sip of his tea and bowed. "Okay, you got *me*. I'm on a scouting mission. Ben and Liddy and..."

"And Heather and Nick. Right. The Heterosexual Power Cabal wants to know my business." Jim tried not to blush, but the heat in his cheeks told him he was losing that war. "Send out an e-mail, tell everyone I had a nice birthday, okay?"

Terry seemed pleased and content with this answer and rolled back, cackling intermittently as he turned on his computer.

Jim wondered how many e-mails he was going to get that were the equivalent of getting a high five in the gym.

The truth was, he had more than a nice birthday. Nice dinner, nice guy, great sex, and a kiss at his door that rattled his brain cells. All that he could probably deal with, but the truth was, he was way beyond that right now. Griffin was still at his apartment. They'd talked briefly about meeting for lunch. Now Jim sat at his desk, less than an hour after leaving, wondering if Griffin would stay another night.

Another night.

As in a two-night stand.

He should be more terrified than this.

Then his phone beeped. And beeped again. And again. A quick scroll of the messages revealed some nonverbal high fives and a little smiley face laughing at him from Mimi.

Gosh, he was so glad to provide entertainment for the Cabal.

* * *

Jim and Terry ended up on a homicide for most of the afternoon and lunch was some burgers at a drive-through. He managed to call Griffin in the middle of all the chaos at the apartment building where a drug deal had gone bad. With-a-machete bad.

When Griffin offered casually to stay until Jim got off work, Jim had a thousand good reasons to shoot this down, to tell him to go back to Hollywood, but he ended up asking Griffin if he liked Italian and could he grab a bottle of wine from the store around the corner.

Later, as he and Terry drove back to the station, Jim tried to mentally blame the seemingly permanent misplacement of his guard on old age. Or loneliness. It'd been a few months since Ben had moved out. He didn't have anyone to come home to; sex aside, sometimes it was just nice to eat leftovers with another human being while you watched ESPN.

Then work boiled up again, and Jim went from his desk to the interrogation room down to Narcotics and back again until Terry announced it was time to go.

And for once, Jim didn't feel like arguing. Instead he shut down his computer and called Direnzo's from his cell to order ahead of time. He went a little overboard on the amount of food, not giving the conversation a second thought until he hung up and saw Terry's wide-eyed look from over the divider.

"Wait… You…you just ordered for at least two people. Do you have plans again tonight?" Terry was well and truly shocked by this amazing development.

Jim pocketed his cell and put on his jacket, head ducked to avoid any eye contact.

"Yeah, actually."

"Wait—is this with the same guy?"

"Yeah, actually." Jim rolled his chair under his desk and headed for the door, Terry at his heels.

"Wait—so he stayed, at your apartment, and he's…staying another night?"

Jim might have announced that he and bigfoot were expecting a baby given Terry's breathless shock. He hit the elevator button impatiently.

"Yes." Jim tapped his foot, then reached over to punch Terry in the arm when he started snickering. "And don't even think of texting Mimi so she can harass me."

"Can I tell her when I get home? She's going to be delighted."

"Oh yes, please share more details of my personal life with your wife. I know I'm like a hobby to her."

"Now, Jim, she just wants you to be happy…"

They got on the elevator, and Jim sighed with begrudging acceptance.

"Yeah, I know. I know you and Mimi and Heather and Nick and Ben and Liddy are wanting the best for me… I just don't want you all holding your breath waiting for me to end up like you."

"You mean heterosexual or happily married?"

"I don't want to get married."

"Well, we've discussed it, and we'll all settle for happy."

* * *

Jim said good-bye to Terry and drove over to the restaurant to pick up dinner. Terry's words stuck with him the entire way.

His friends wanted him to be happy—they wanted it passionately and sincerely and with great gusto. And that level of enthusiasm really brought the point home as to how miserable his world must look from the outside.

And God knew he tried to pretend it didn't suck most of the time, but that was getting more and more difficult. He may tease the Heterosexual Power Cabal, but ultimately they had people to go home to, people to share their lives with, and he had...nothing. An unrequited crush, a lot of anonymous shit in bars he was way too old for, and his only real family was a guy spending his days planning for the rapidly approaching end.

Is that what he was doing in his own way?

Heavy shit weighing on his mind as he parked and went in to pay for the meal. The three bags threw fantastic smells in his direction as he waited for his credit card to go through; the girl behind the counter was clearly one of Dom's many teenage granddaughters. They were like black-haired, brown-eyed clones with dimples, seemingly churned out in the back along with great garlic bread and killer lasagna.

Jim tipped her ten bucks and took a few moments to be pleased at how happy she looked.

In the truck, Jim dialed Griffin's cell phone.

"Hello?"

"Hi, it's me. Jim. I'm on my way. Just picked up dinner…" Jim cleared his throat.

"Great! I'm starving. God, this is an amazing neighborhood," Griffin said exuberantly. "I went to get the wine and stayed out for like three hours. I even got some writing done."

Jim was pleased that Griffin liked his neighborhood, pleased that Griffin seemed to have enjoyed his day so much.

"That sounds like a nice day. I'll…uh, be there in about ten minutes."

"Cool. See you then."

Griffin hung up, and Jim stared at the phone for a second.

That was…borderline domestic.

* * *

Jim took the elevator up, holding the bags of dinner, his bag over one shoulder. He swallowed as he glanced in the narrow mirrored panels, a distorted reflection of someone who appeared to look a bit like James Shea and yet not at all.

Particularly the expression of anticipation.

The doors opened into his loft, and he heard some Miles Davis piped through the sound system he rarely used; apparently Griffin had done some exploring, which would be worrisome if Jim had anything interesting hidden anywhere.

"Hey, I hope you don't mind. This place was way too quiet," Griffin called.

"No problem." It's nice, Jim thought as he walked into the kitchen. Griffin was pouring wine in two large glasses that Jim didn't recognize, mostly because he didn't have wineglasses.

"You didn't have wineglasses." Griffin smiled, handing him a glass. "Take off your coat, stay awhile."

"What? Oh yeah." Jim lost the work bag, the parcels of dinner, his jacket, and his shoes, and returned to the island where his wine waited.

Griffin dug into the bags, making little comments about great smells and enough food for lumberjacks. Jim sipped his wine, absorbed the jazz, and slid onto one of the bar stools to relax his back.

"You look like you had an ass kicker of a day."

"Yeah." He sighed deeply without meaning to.

"Why don't you take a shower? I'll dish up dinner, and we'll just hang out." Griffin was already in the cabinets, pulling out dishes and silverware with complete ease.

More at ease than Jim usually was in his own home.

"How do you do that?"

"What?" Griffin was wearing a pair of jeans and an undershirt, his round, intellectual writer glasses perched on his nose. He looked casual from the inside out, completely tuned in to Jim and dinner and this moment. Jim identified the emotion under his skin at the moment as jealousy.

"You're just…" Jim gestured at him. "You're so good at this."

"Good at?" Griffin looked at the dishes in his hand. "Good at setting the table? My dad made me do it every night. He didn't want me to think it was woman's work." He laughed.

"Progressive dad?"

"My dad raised eight daughters and one son by himself. He had eleven sisters. When I tell you my dad is a feminist, I mean that from his very core he had absolute knowledge and respect of strong-minded women," Griffin said drily.

"Impressive."

"Yeah, very much so." Griffin put the dishes on the table. "But did you mean my domestic skills or something else?"

Jim toyed with the wineglass. "I couldn't do this. Like— stay over and be comfortable and hang out and…keep going."

Griffin shrugged, and Jim saw his embarrassment. "Should I be apologizing and calling a cab? Because if I'm overstaying my welcome, dude, kick my ass to the curb."

"You're not! No, no, that's not what I mean." Jim stood up, nervous that he was blowing this thing that he couldn't define but wasn't ready to give up. "I'm…impressed and a little jealous, okay? I like it. It's just completely different from what I'm used to, so, you know—slight freak-out."

"Oh, okay." Griffin started to pace the small space between the sink and stove and the corner of the island. "You know, because I had this freak-out already this afternoon. When I said I'd stay and then I thought—what the fuck? Seriously? Dude, get a plane ticket."

"You don't have to leave…"

"Good, because I'm starving." Griffin looked a little sheepish. "And I, uh—I got some writing done, and that hasn't happened in a while."

Jim nodded, going back to his wine—then turned around. "Wait, you said the screenplay was almost done…"

"Oh, right." Griffin pinkened. "I totally bullshitted you on that."

"Anything else I should know you bullshitted me on?" Jim gave him the one-eyebrow quirk.

"I'm not usually that phenomenal in bed?"

"I don't believe that for a second," Jim said breezily, taking the glass and heading for the bathroom. "How good are you in the shower?"

"Blurry, because I can't wear my glasses or my contacts—but I'm pretty sure I can find your dick without much problem."

"That's all I need to know."

* * *

Dinner waited. They ate warmed-up pasta and sausage and garlic bread on the couch, wrapped in towels in an entangled sprawl. Miles kept singing all his greatest hits—

and there were, luckily, hours of them, since neither man was inclined to move anytime soon to change the CDs.

"This is nice," Griffin said, so quietly that Jim nearly missed it. They were shoulder to shoulder, and the food coma had hit Griffin first. He sounded sleepy and content, dropping his damp curls back onto the couch.

"Very nice," Jim agreed, his voice hushed from disuse.

"I can't see anything."

"Your eyes are closed."

"I mean—I don't have my glasses."

"Still in the bathroom?"

"Yeah."

Jim wrestled himself out of the cushions and Griffin's warm comfort. He cleaned up the dishes, left everything in the sink for later, and put the leftovers away. In the bathroom, he tidied up and realized he was cold—that meant a quick jog up the loft stairs to get some sweats, then another trip back up when he wondered if Griffin might be cold, so he grabbed another pair and a blanket from the closet.

When he got back to the couch, Griffin was sideways, curled into an S with his head on one of the throw pillows. The towel had loosened, showing off one muscular thigh and a ghost of his hip. Sound asleep.

Jim drank it in. For however long this little fantasy of perfect domestication lasted, he was going to savor it. When it evaporated later or tomorrow or whenever, he'd have memories to last him through the next drought.

Which, by his calculations, was twenty-five-or-so years long if he was judging by the last one.

Jim laid the sweats over the back of the couch, the glasses within easy reach on the table, and tucked the blanket around Griffin's shoulders and down over his body. One smoothing touch to his hair and Jim felt his chest tighten.

This guy was entirely too easy to like and too easy to get used to. He already hated the part where it was going to have to end.

Chapter Thirteen

When he started getting the "*wtf r u?*" texts from Daisy forty-eight hours after their last phone call, Griffin knew he was in trouble. And he knew he had to pick up the phone and call her—and ask if she could get her housekeeper to go over and water his fern, collect his mail, and take out the garbage.

He needed to go home at some point. And for the past three days, he'd thought of bringing it up to Jim again—just to get a sense if that first night's coolness had extended a few more days. But then Griffin realized that *Jim* hadn't brought it up again either. And if Jim wasn't bringing it up and it was his place, then Griffin didn't see the need to bring it up.

He knew they were using the script as an excuse and even talked about it here and there to justify his continued presence, but ultimately, this was one long-ass date, with dinners and sex and walks and sex and basketball games on the television followed by sex.

If they truly discussed it, the bubble would burst and reality—that dreaded sonofabitch—would park itself in the living room and that would be it.

Griffin wasn't ready for "it" yet.

He put the load of laundry in the dryer (and yeah, he did Jim's—so what, it was his apartment and it was just *nice manners*) and ran the sponge over the counter again, unnecessarily. Out of chores and excuses, Griffin grabbed his BlackBerry and headed for the balcony, spreading out on one of the Adirondack chairs Jim had out there.

The Seattle skyline and some puffy white clouds against the gray-hued afternoon sky settled his nerves until the phone started ringing and Daisy picked up immediately.

Christ, he was in so much trouble.

"Where the hell are you?" she said by way of greeting, and Griffin sighed.

"Still in Seattle."

"*What?*"

"What what?" he asked, suddenly defensive instead of his planned apologetics. "I'm in Seattle."

"With Jim." Not a question.

"Yeah, with Jim."

"You've been there almost a week—what the hell are you doing?" Her shrill voice had an edge to it, and only someone who'd known her as long as he had would detect the fear under the growing temper tantrum.

"It's been less than four days, and I'm having a nice time, actually—thanks for asking."

Silence filled the line and went a few seconds past surprise into something else.

"What are you two, like a couple or something now?"

"No!" Griffin sputtered out a laugh. "Seriously, Daisy Mae—it's been like three nights. That's not a relationship, that's a long-ass date. We're just having a good time. No big deal." Every word was the truth and a big fat lie; Griffin hoped Daisy was too caught up in her own drama to scent that out.

"Your MO isn't really no big deal, Griff. You went for one night, I was thinking to get laid, shore up the deal, and now this," she said, her voice dropping to a dangerous quiet. "We've been here before, Griffin, and it didn't end well."

Griffin couldn't muster enough balls to call her on the implication that this time it wasn't him whoring for the movie deal.

"No, it's not a replay of anything. We're just hanging out, no strings attached."

He heard murmurs through the line—Daisy talking to herself. He could sense the precipice, the moment between Daisy going ballistic and Daisy backing down. It could go either way.

"I'm sorry," she said finally, her soft "forgive me" voice sweet in his ear. "I just got worried, okay? You're never gone like this without calling me or at least a text. I was concerned."

"Well, then I'm sorry too, okay? I just got caught up in writing and this little minivacation," he murmured, relieved to avoid a fight. "I didn't mean to drop out of sight."

"Do you know when you're coming back? I mean, just asking because Claus is having a party at the Four Seasons for Lina Devore…" Her voice trailed off, and Griffin rubbed his eyes under his glasses. Claus's newest mistress, a French actress who had about as much talent as Pepe Le Pew but a hell of a rack—Daisy's newest replacement.

Sick cycle. Claus loved the roller coaster, Daisy always had a reason not to get off, and Griffin wanted to punch Claus's stupid face in because he couldn't be mad at Daisy.

"When's the party? I'll make sure I'm back and we'll go together, okay?" he assured her, guilt eating his guts. "Do you have a new dress?"

Daisy sighed. "No, not yet. Jules is bringing some things over today."

"Send me pictures on my phone. We'll pick out something fantastic. No one will notice the French tickler."

"You're mean," Daisy said, but he heard the lightening of her voice. "I love you. And I really am sorry, Griff. I swear. I was a total brat, but you know, there's just a lot…"

"Don't apologize, okay? It's partially my fault for being so amazing you can't do without me," he teased.

"That's not even a real joke," she said.

"I know; I am amazing. Now go have a soak, and I'll be waiting for cleavage shots."

"Love you, Griff."

"Love you too, Daisy Mae."

* * *

After the phone call with Daisy, Griffin sat in apparently the only beam of sunlight in Seattle, conveniently pointed to the chair on Jim's balcony.

Oh yes, they'd been here before, back when Griffin was young and stupid, or at least younger and more stupid. He'd ditched reality and fallen hard and fast on more than one occasion, and every time, Daisy was there to remind him of the facts.

Daisy ripped him more than one new one about men and their asshole ways and their "newer, better, shinier" needs. He always knew she was ranting about Claus, but then again, she wasn't wrong.

"*Don't get comfortable. It'll never be what you think it is.*"

* * *

Griffin folded the laundry, sick to his stomach.

Jim was a repressed workaholic who didn't date, who didn't have real relationships. Here comes Griffin, willing to do whatever he wanted to make him a happy little home. Dinner on the table? A good fucking? Fun conversation? No problem! Can I roll over and fetch your slippers while I'm at it? Thank you for not throwing me out—yet!

Any day now, Jim would come home in a foul mood and decide he didn't want to have some stranger in his space. And that would be that. This illusion would be blown to shit and Griffin would be on another plane, in another limo with Daisy's stony, self-righteous anger simmering in the air.

And she would be right again.

* * *

Griffin packed his bag in Jim's bedroom.

He was deciding between a text message and a note for Jim, something simple about "thanks for the fun and see you later and it was *great*," or maybe that wasn't cool and detached enough. It had to be casual, because he couldn't jeopardize the movie.

Griffin was terrible at casual, as was clearly demonstrated by how long it took to pack up a pair of underwear, socks, jeans, and a T-shirt.

It took him so long, in fact, he realized the shadows had gotten longer and more pronounced. His stomach growled defiantly at the lack of lunch or dinner, and he checked the clock on the nightstand.

Jim would be home any minute.

The BlackBerry buzzed next to him. It was a text message from Jim.

Griffin stomach did a mighty flip as he pressed the Accept button.

Feel like going out? Meet me downstairs in thirty.

Daisy could be right tomorrow; he texted back *yes* and unpacked his bag. For now.

Chapter Fourteen

"That lobster was amazing," Griffin said as the truck pulled into Jim's regular parking space.

"Yeah, the decor isn't much, but the food's out of this world." Jim put the truck into park and sighed as he shut the engine off. He was bone-weary tired and putting off a very pressing question about how long Griffin was staying.

Because on one hand—no complaints. On the other hand—it was starting to be a "thing," and Jim was terrible at "things."

"Tired?" Griffin laid his hand against the back of Jim's neck as he rested his head against the steering wheel.

He tried not to purr.

"Uh-huh."

"We should have stayed in, then."

We.

Jim shrugged, pulling himself together as he sat up. He shot Griffin a nervous smile in the dark.

"Thought I should show you all the nice Seattle spots before you went home."

Uncomfortable silence followed his words, his words that he wanted to suck back in because that wasn't how he wanted to do this at all.

"Oh right...about that." Griffin was reaching for the door handle now, hands to himself. "I talked to Daisy earlier—we have this party...thing...to go to this weekend..."

"Of course. I'm surprised you haven't had anything better to do in the past week..." Oh God. Jim clamped his mouth shut. He was making this worse.

"Glamorous life of a movie star's gay companion—party after party," Griffin said sarcastically, getting out of the truck and slamming the door.

"What?" Jim grabbed his keys and hauled out of the truck after him. "I didn't say that. I was just...wondering."

"Wondering what? Why I didn't seem to have a life to go back to? I've been writing, okay? A lot of writing. That's what I do. I can do it anywhere, and here is where it's working." Griffin's furious pace into the building was curtailed by Jim's fumbling with the keys.

"Okay, okay." Jim opened the door, and Griffin pushed inside, stalking to the elevator. "I'm sorry. I was just making conversation."

"Moronic conversation," Griffin muttered, tapping his foot against the floor, waiting for Jim to produce the elevator key. "If you want me out, just say so."

"I didn't say that."

"You might as well have. Sorry, I thought you were having fun."

"*I am.*"

"Then why are you shoving me out the door?" Griffin was yelling now, and Jim felt his own temperature rise. Yeah, this was why he didn't do dating anymore. Fucking drama.

"You said you had a party to fly down for, I was wondering why you hadn't had anything else—that's it. *You* brought up leaving." Jim slammed into the elevator and punched the button.

Griffin folded his arms over his chest and stared at the shiny slivers of glass in the elevator. He didn't look at Jim, didn't acknowledge his words—nothing except the muscle in his jaw that kept jumping.

Jim stared at that.

"It's no big deal," Griffin said suddenly as the doors opened. "This wasn't anything but like...hanging out and fucking. Whatever. I should be able to get a flight first thing in the morning."

"Right," Jim answered but then wondered why the hell they were fighting about something that wasn't a big deal. That was stupid. This was stupid. "Whatever you want to do."

"Right. Whatever."

"Right. *Whatever.*" Jim threw his hands up, and his keys went flying.

Griffin was muttering again as he stalked outside onto the balcony.

"For the love of..." Jim started stripping out of his work clothes, heading upstairs to get something to change into.

Maybe go for a run, because there would be no peaceful evening of hanging out with someone (and sex, couldn't forget the sex), because that was shot.

He reached the top of the stairs, and all his thoughts grounded to a halt as he spied the folded clothes on his bed.

It took a second, but then he recognized them as his. As in formerly dirty clothes washed and neatly folded in a stack on the made bed.

He blinked, then leaned over to look at the rest of the loft below.

Clean. Tidied up. He thought for sure he'd left some junk mail on the counter this morning and a few dishes in the sink, but no. Everything was neat as a pin. He spotted a new box of cereal on the counter. Dish soap—he'd forgotten that during his last trip to the twenty-four-hour market.

Griffin, in a few short days, might be the best roommate he had ever had.

Roommate with benefits.

It made him tired to think about how accustomed he'd gotten to the other man in less than a week. And then he was tired and afraid, at the prospect of coming home tomorrow and not being able to see Griffin.

Stupid. This shouldn't have happened, bad idea. Very bad. Complicated like Jim didn't remember how to handle.

"Hey, Jim?" Griffin's voice reached him, and he turned around to find him half-way up on the stairs, looking as crappy as he felt.

"Thanks for doing my laundry." Blurting out the first thing in his head wasn't Jim's best bet most of the time, but it seemed to momentarily bring a smile to Griffin's face.

"Oh, no problem. I was doing mine…" His voice trailed off as he looked around the loft, carefully avoiding resting his gaze on the bed. "Anyway, I just wanted to apologize for picking a stupid fight. Me and Daisy had a thing on the phone, and I was feeling—" Griffin made a gesture with his hand. "I was feeling like a fuckup so, you know, acted like one. Completing the asshole circle." He punctuated it with a circling of his hands in the air.

Jim sat down on the bed, all confusion and a loss of words.

"So let's pretend I don't know what I'm doing here, or what I'm doing wrong actually."

Griffin came up the last few steps and settled on the top stair, watching Jim warily. "You didn't do anything wrong. I'm some guy who pushed his way into a dinner date, then boom! I never leave!"

"It's only a few days." But that didn't make sense, because really—who did this? Jim never did it. "It's not like you moved in."

"I did laundry here."

"You did my laundry! That was—Thank you. It was very nice," Jim pointed out, hands clasped between his knees.

"It's weird."

"Why is it weird? I've had roommates who never did that." Even Ben never did his laundry, and he spent a long time imagining himself in love with *him.*

"It's not really a roommate thing," Griffin said, a confused expression settling on his face. "It's like a... a...boyfriend thing. Haven't you ever lived with a boyfriend who did your laundry?"

Jim thought about it, then thought it was weird he had to think about it. Wasn't there a quick memory that popped into his head?

Nope, nothing.

"No. I've lived with boyfriends, but none of them did much of anything."

Wow, he had terrible taste in men.

"Well, that's..." Whatever Griffin was going to say was cut off, and Jim watched the emotions play over his face. If this were an interrogation, he'd have wondered what new information was about to come to light.

"What? Proof my past relationships probably sucked. Because they did."

"No." Griffin frowned. "Yes. I mean, I was going to say yeah, that sucks, and then I remembered being the person who does all of that without reciprocation sucks too." He shrugged.

"So, uh—you're regretting doing my laundry?" Jim rubbed his forehead. This was an excellent reminder of how soulless sex was so much easier than conversation. "Because, you know—I'm good with you not doing it when you're here. But if you want to, it's really nice."

Griffin smirked. "Good God, are you this ridiculous with suspects?"

"No, I'm actually great at that! Witnesses too."

"So this would be going better if I were traumatized or in handcuffs?"

Jim laughed, an honest, amused sound as he shook his head. Yeah, this would be easier in either of those cases, which made him a good cop and a lousy noncop.

"We're quite the pair," Griffin commented as he stood up, stretched out the kinks from his uncomfortable perch. He glanced at the spot on the bed next to Jim—who nodded at both the statement and the unspoken request.

"You're not so bad."

"Thanks, neither are you." Griffin sat down.

"Wanna…I don't know. Do something?"

Griffin raised an eyebrow.

Jim rolled his eyes. "I didn't mean that. I meant…I don't know. Go for a run or a movie. Something."

The other man laughed. "Oddly enough, I never really go to movies and I only run when chased."

"What about all those premieres?"

"Dude, you never actually watch the movie. You do the red carpet, hang out in the VIP room and drink, then go to the party afterward and tell everyone how much you loved the movie."

Jim shook his head. "That makes absolutely no sense."

"It's Hollywood. It's not supposed to make sense." Griffin paused. "Actually it might be nice to see a movie without pressure to make up something nice about it."

"If you hate it, I promise not to be upset," Jim said drily. He looked over at his dresser. "Lemme change, you check the paper for the movie times."

"I have my BlackBerry."

"Riiiight. Whatever; check the thing that tells you when the next showing of whatever movie you want to see is, and I'll change into roomier pants."

"Roomy?"

"Popcorn."

* * *

They ended up at a ten p.m. showing of a sequel to a movie neither of them saw the original of, but Griffin knew the director and insisted it would be brainless crap and easy to follow. He wasn't wrong.

They shared a giant popcorn, and Jim made it to the last scene without falling asleep—a major accomplishment for him. As everyone filed out, Griffin remained in his seat, however, even as Jim was standing up.

"What are you waiting for?" Jim yawned, dusting kernels off his pants.

"Watching the credits."

"That was a terrible movie. Are you looking for people to blame?"

"Noooo—all these people worked hard for this terrible movie. It's their job." Griffin looked embarrassed as the lights came up, so Jim sat back down.

"So you watch the credits?

"Every movie, every television show. 'Cause—you know, someone should." Griffin rolled his eyes and shook his head. "Okay, I've never said that out loud before, and it sounds ridiculous—let's go."

Jim shook his head. He'd never thought about it that way. They were just credits; he never related them to actual people. People like Griffin. "Nah, let's stay. Hey, we should watch one of your movies so I can see your name."

"My stuff kinda sucks."

"I thought you were successful." Jim's gaze narrowed. Ed's movie shouldn't be in the hands of anyone who sucks. "Daisy is…"

"Daisy is a movie star. I make a living at what I do. Neither necessarily equals high quality. I mean—Twinkies sell more than gourmet chocolates."

"Twinkies are *good*. They…hit the spot. Sometimes you don't want gourmet."

"Yeah, sometimes you want synthetic crap that will survive the apocalypse."

"Nothing wrong with that."

"That's debatable." Griffin wasn't looking at him; his eyes were on the screen, and Jim wasn't sure he was still focusing on the people behind the names. "Sometimes I'd like to be doing a bit…more."

"Like Ed's movie? Is that what this is about? A side project—that's what you called it at dinner the other night."

"Yeah. Yeah." Griffin sighed as he turned to face Jim. "Listen, you have to know—we're not going to screw Ed over. I absolutely swear it. Daisy and I are taking this very seriously, not just because of the subject matter but because in all honest selfishness...this is our big chance to prove we're not just...Twinkies."

"That doesn't sound so bad." Jim rubbed his hands on his pants. "It's not, is it?"

"No, it's not. Nothing is bad about this. Daisy and I are just trying to make a bit more out of our lives and..." Another sigh. "Just trying for more, you know?"

"Okay." The credits had stopped and given way to a static advertisement for a local car dealership. "So you and Daisy, you're quite the package deal."

The casual, concerned tone of Jim's voice got Griffin's attention. His eyes widened, and the frown teasing the corners of his mouth was impossible to miss. "She's my best friend."

"Right, I got that." The employees wandered in, sweeping up the dregs of the crowd. Jim knew they were the last people there and should get the hell out, but this seemed too important a moment to delay. "I just mean—you work together, you hang out together..."

"Nothing's going on," Griffin said defensively. "If that's what you're worried about."

"No, no. Wasn't going there. You told me you had no interest in her lady parts, and I believe you."

"Thank you; I appreciate you believing I'm gay." Griffin gathered up his empty cup and Raisinet box and stood up to go. "So what—don't you spend a lot of time with your friends?"

"Well—actually." Jim stood and shuffled down the aisle.

"Lemme guess: not a lot of friends."

"It's more a casual cop thing, and uh—okay, there's the Power Cabal."

"Excuse me?" Griffin tossed his trash away and faced Jim in the lobby, a confused expression on his face. "Oh God, you're not in some weird cult, are you? Or one of those vigilante groups that goes after criminals who aren't convicted."

Jim shook his head. "Wait—I've seen that movie."

"Michaels Douglas, Hal Holbrook. Frickin' brilliant." Griffin wiped his hands on his jeans. "What were we talking about again?"

"I don't have a clue."

They made it out to the parking lot before Griffin snapped his fingers. "What the hell is the Power Cabal anyway?"

"Oh." Jim opened the door for Griffin, feeling embarrassed about calling his friends that out loud. "It's three couples—my partner and his wife. My ex-roommate and his wife. Two people from the prosecutor's office—they're getting married in a few months. Anyway, they have dinner together once a month, on a Friday, and I always get invited and—well, they're great people, but it's like hanging out with six grandmas who are trying to get you married off as soon as possible."

Griffin slipped into the truck, clearly trying to hold back his laughter. "Your friends are a bunch of hetero yentas? Seriously? Jim, you haven't stopped surprising me yet."

"They're very good people," Jim said, almost defensively. He started up the truck. "They're almost all—Well, Terry worked with me on the case. Nick and Heather were the prosecutors on Ed's daughter's case."

Griffin perked up. "Huh. I should probably meet them. When's the next dinner?"

"No."

"No?"

"No. No way. I've never brought a guy with me, and I never will. They'll be all over you—seriously, you have no idea."

"It's a research project! For the movie! You could just tell them I'm a writer…"

"Terry knows."

"Terry—your partner, knows what?"

"That we've been…that you've been here."

"Uh-huh."

"At my apartment with me!"

"So your partner knows you slept with me, and that means I can't go to dinner with you?"

"If you met my friends, you'd understand."

"But I can't meet your friends," Griffin said drily.

"That was a rhetorical statement."

Griffin snickered, then made chicken sounds under his breath for the rest of the ride home.

Chapter Fifteen

Griffin pushed his sunglasses onto the top of his head as he maneuvered poolside at Claus and Daisy's party. The Four Seasons had been unable to comply with all Claus's demands, so the event for his new girlfriend had been relocated to the Bel Air mansion he and his wife shared.

Fucked up, Hollywood-style.

The Nirvana T-shirt, disreputable jeans, and flip-flops were Griffin's way of giving Claus the middle finger and also helpful when he needed to duck into a crowd of servers and catch his breath.

He felt like he'd been away from this shit for months instead of a few days. Seattle felt like a pull at the back of his mind; LA felt like a stranger.

The crowd currently eating lettuce wraps and sucking down pomegranate martinis comprised the early birds, those with better places to be in an hour, personal assistants who got on the list as a favor from their bosses (and were excellent gossip conduits), and a smattering of folks who lived for spectacles like this.

It was like NASCAR for the rich and famous; if they were really lucky, there would be a wreck, like Daisy getting drunk and throwing Lina in the pool.

Griffin, of course, was there out of love and to be moral support. And to stop Lina from being drowned in the hot tub.

"Griffin!" He heard an Australian lilt to his name and turned with a smile; Jules, Daisy's long-suffering assistant, was headed his way, two giant margaritas in hand.

"Those both for me?"

"God, no, you need to fetch your own, darling. Herr Claus is in a *mood*, and Daisy's being a wee bitchy herself. I'm going to need both of these to get through the next hour," she said drily, then took a long sip as punctuation.

"Give me a number on the Richter scale, please." Griffin ignored her as he snatched one of the elaborate drinks for himself.

"He's a twelve, she's a five. I got her dressed, gave her a Valium, and made her eat. We should be okay so long as Claus doesn't fuck Lina on the diving board."

"I really think having the three of them around a large pool of water is a terrible idea."

"Oh, I don't know. A few banana peels and all our problems could be solved."

"Jules!" Griffin tsk-tsked at her.

"What?"

"Not enough salt," he said, gesturing at the glass.

* * *

After one drink and a nice conversation with Jules, Griffin felt fortified enough to seek out Daisy and potentially brush past Claus—who would completely ignore him.

In the pool house, he found his friend pacing in circles around the small bedroom, heels clicking on the wooden floor. From the tight clutch of her hands against her chest, he imagined this had been going on since Jules left.

Griffin plastered a smile on his face and pushed the door open, knocking as he went.

"Gorgeous girl! I told you the pink was perfection." He opened his arms and braced himself for impact when Daisy ran to give him a hug.

"You're late, but I forgive you." She sniffled theatrically, avoiding his white shirt with her heavily made-up face. "You smell funny."

"Compliments will get you everywhere. Also? Jules forced me to drink a margarita."

"She gave me a Valium. And a banana."

"I win!"

Daisy laughed, and it was a real laugh, not the fake dazzle charm she did for the media or the various hangers-on who made their living off her talent. He'd never wanted to sleep with Daisy, but he liked being the only one to make her happy.

"Come on, you need to make a grand entrance and have people eating out of the palm of your hand before whatshername and Claus trip in."

Her thousand-watt smile dimmed slightly. "Claus is in a terrible mood. He fired Nico Watts."

The writer doing Lina's debut film. Griffin shrugged. "What? He use too many two-syllable words for her to learn?"

"He didn't say. He just hated the script and threw it in the fireplace, and then fired him."

"Nico will shortly look back on this firing as the best thing that ever happened to him. And Claus will find another desperate screenwriter to pull together some crap for the French whore."

"I don't know." Daisy bit her lip. "What if he asks you?"

Griffin laughed and shook his head. "He can't afford me."

"Your contract…"

"Says I have to write movies for Bright Side. Claus isn't going to waste me on Lina and her soft-core, straight-to-DVD debut."

"Okay." Daisy didn't seem to believe him. Maybe she was remembering, as he was, her own straight-to-VHS debut all those years ago. "Should we go out?"

"Yes, yes, we should. Maybe Jules will get us more margaritas."

* * *

Daisy clung to Griffin's arm until they came into sight of the party; then she quickly let go. He knew she had to appear in control and blithely ignoring the whole ugly mess when Claus arrived with Lina. So he trailed behind, signaling Jules across the patio, who quickly grabbed some margaritas and headed their way.

"Thank you," Daisy said sweetly as Griffin gave Jules a wink. He knew that her drink would be mild so as not to play havoc with the Valium.

"Mine better be a double," he murmured, and Jules smirked at him, straightening her square black glasses.

"Triple," she whispered back as she moved to stand next to Daisy, ever present and alert. "Everything's taken care of. I double-checked with the caterer. Just let me know when you want to set out the food…"

"Have the valet at the gate text you when Claus pulls up and set the food out then." Daisy smiled, stirring her glass and calling out hellos to passing guests.

"So everyone will have their mouths full when the French tickler shows up," Griffin said. "Clever girl."

Daisy shrugged, but her semievil grin said everything. "I'm going to mingle. Let me know when he shows up, all right?"

"Of course," Jules said as Daisy swished off, her long maxi dress brushing over her cork platforms. She looked like the perfect hostess, carefree and beautiful as she surveyed the fruits of her career.

Griffin sucked down the rest of his margarita, getting a head rush for his trouble. Daisy was in "fuck you" mode, which meant he and Jules might be very busy later.

"Are there paps here?"

"The usual invitees, but we've got like five people on the list who smell fishy to me." Jules pursed her very red lips. Dressed all in black with short, spiked blonde hair, she looked painfully out of place at this party; in reality, she was probably the only person even remotely together on the premises.

"Undercover paps, Herr Claus, the French whore, and Daisy. Around a large pool of water. This might be better than that Aspen trip where Claus brought Hedda and Daisy had too much cognac…"

Jules shuddered. "We swore to never speak of that again."

* * *

Eventually Jules had to make her dutiful rounds, and Griffin was left alone in a shadowy corner of the elaborate stone patio, sitting on a low-lying wall surrounded by red waxy flowers he couldn't identify. No one was interested in getting his ear at the moment, and truth be told, he saw no one he was interested in getting the ear of. So he sat and drank the dregs of his drink, thinking about how much he didn't want to be here and spending a brief amount of time admitting to himself where he *did* want to be.

In Seattle, at Jim's sterile loft.

Leaving proved more difficult than he imagined, their few days together a comfortable routine he hated to break out of. Even Jim seemed blue about the whole thing—which was both incredibly fabulous and incredibly unsettling.

No one said anything about Griffin coming back, but he felt like it was unspoken. They'd of course have to meet more regarding the screenplay, and Griffin sensed Jim wouldn't mind a return "date."

But being manly jerks, they left it at "see you soon" and that was that.

Griffin wondered if twenty-eight hours was too early to call or text.

Was there a *Cosmo* article about this?

Could he Google an answer?

"Screw it," he muttered. It was the weekend—Jim would probably be out and about doing "single cop with no social life" things. He would most likely get voice mail…

As the house phone rang, Griffin had second thoughts, but the "hello?" at the other end made him smile too much to remember he was nervous.

"Hey, it's me. Griffin." He cleared his throat. "So I'm sitting at this glamorous Hollywood party and bored stupid. Entertain me."

Jim laughed through the phone, and Griffin ducked his head to hide the bursting grin across his face.

"My singing voice is terrible, and I don't know any jokes."

"Sad, very sad. Okay, then, tell me about your day."

"That might be even sadder. I went for a run, did an hour at the gym, cleaned the loft, and went to the grocery store."

"Did you buy for more than one day?"

"Yes, I actually did. I used a cart, even. I thought the cashier was going to need smelling salts."

"I'm very impressed!"

"Thank you. When, uh, when you get back up here, I'll cook something for you."

There was an awkward silence, and Griffin shuffled his feet to hide his absolute delight.

"That sounds nice," Griffin said, clearing his throat. "I was thinking—you know, to be honest, I got more written at your place than I've done at my own in ages…"

"So you coming up here would be good. For the screenplay."

"Right, exactly. And I'd love to drive up to see Ed at some point. We could, uh, do that together."

"Sure. Absolutely." Jim coughed. "So, you know, just let me know when you're coming up—to work on the screenplay, and I'll leave you a spare set of keys."

"And cook for me."

"Right…and cook for you." He laughed again, and Griffin wanted to keep score. Relaxed, honest laughter—twice in one five-minute conversation.

"I gotta see what's going on here in la-la land, but maybe Tuesday."

"Tuesday is good. I might have off on Thursday, so we can drive up to Ed's Wednesday night."

"Perfect."

Griffin heard Jules's voice over the sound system, calling everyone to the buffet. Which meant Claus and the whore were on their way, and Daisy would be buzzing like a bug zapper.

"Sorry, I have to run. Dinner is being served, and there's a whole big Daisy thing…"

"Sure, no problem. I'm gonna go steam the floors."

"You're a party animal, Jim."

"Have fun."

Griffin snapped his phone off and got up, then dodged the queuing crowd as they headed for the overstuffed buffet tables set up near the main house. Waiters in smart red polo shirts helped people with serving; Griffin thought it looked like a posh episode of *Star Trek*. Red shirts and lobster. He wondered which one might get caught in the middle of a claw-to-claw battle between Claus's women tonight.

"Where's Daisy Mae?" he asked, catching up with Jules near the head of the tables.

"She's holding court with a group of—I don't know— male underwear models? No clue. They're all young and pretty, however, and God, someone tell her to not hike her dress so high," Jules muttered, holding her walkie-talkie up to listen to the squawk from the head valet. "Claus and Lina are on their way through the house."

"Crap, I should have drunk more..." Griffin checked his hair and the collar of his shirt in Jules's glasses until she smacked him in the chest.

"Go run interference while I keep the line moving," she muttered, gesturing him toward Daisy, her high-pitched laughter hurting both their ears.

"Right-o." He snapped a salute and casually sauntered over to where Daisy was perched on a chaise, five equally stunning young men smiling at her attentively in a circle.

"All for me? You shouldn't have," he murmured in her ear as he slid in next to her, wrapping his arm around her shoulders.

"You'll have to share." Daisy pouted pretty, but the reality was that he made it a point to never pick up her disappointed leftovers.

"But of course." Griffin winked at the bronzed Adonis closest to him, who seemed to be checking him out. Okeydoke. "Are you hungry?"

"No, I'm fine." Daisy turned back to the Hispanic lad on her left, who seemed to be staring at Daisy like she was the buffet and he scored the first in line.

He wondered if there were head shots folded into their Speedos for later "dropping off."

"Claus is here," he added against her ear, and she nodded without turning around. Griffin sighed but kept his smile bright, smoothing down the hem of her dress before he stood up. "Gonna mingle," he lied, sidestepping the hunk who clearly considered following. "Later, fellows."

Quickly, before he sent out the wrong signal, Griffin jetted for the dinner line, gaze darting between Daisy—now alone with Juan Carlos or whatever his name was—and the entrance to the party where Claus would be exiting.

It didn't take long. Jules gave him a high sign and boom—there was Claus, all six-five Germanic blondness of him, sweeping onto the patio with a smile on his face and Lina on his arm.

He expected fanfare; he got a few people looking up from their plates.

Almost immediately his face fell, and he scanned the crowd for someone—he knew it would be Daisy—and he knew it wouldn't be good when Claus noticed his wife being entertained near the pool. Forget the fact that the man was standing there with his mistress...

"Crap," Griffin muttered, handing his plate over to a waiter and diving back into the milling crowd. He needed to get between Claus and Daisy as soon as he could.

Chapter Sixteen

"Don't," Jules warned from somewhere behind him, but Griffin kept walking. He stepped into Claus's personal space, blinding smile in place.

"Claus, man, good to see you." Griffin gave Lina a quick glance, but it was clear he was blocking Claus's path and not here to chitchat.

"Excuse me; I'm looking for my wife," Claus said, clearly disinterested.

"She's here, no worries. Just doing some entertaining in your absence." Griffin stuck his hand out toward Lina, a statuesque brunette in half a dress and enough bronzer to turn the pool brown. "Griffin Drake, the most talented screenwriter in Claus's employ, so nice to meet you."

Lina's eyes lit up, and she curved her body toward Griffin as she shook his hand, her bangles clattering together. "So lovely to meet you, Griffin. Are you going to be working with me, then?"

"Oh no, no. Sorry. I'm backed up through the end of the world. Claus never lets me rest. I'm only here because a judge ruled against torturing prisoners of war."

Claus certainly didn't laugh, and Lina just looked confused. Griffin felt his heart beating out of his chest.

Baiting Claus? Really? He was going to be lucky if it wasn't his ass drowned before the end of the night.

"Anywho—the buffet is great, and I will absolutely recommend the margaritas. Have a few; they're wonderful."

Griffin took a step back and prayed heartily that Jules was over by Daisy, keeping her dealings with the playboy in the Speedo as squeaky-clean as possible, but from Claus's growing glare, it wasn't working.

"Lina, tell Griffin all about your ideas for the film. I'm actually thinking he'll be perfect." Claus all but shoved Lina onto Griffin's arm and headed for Daisy.

"Well, shit," he muttered, trying to following without tripping over Lina's long legs.

"Let's go get those drinks," Lina said, her grip strong. Griffin's eyes were on Claus, but Lina's voice whispered to him, "Let it go, okay? We should stay out of the way." Mysteriously, her French accent had disappeared some time before the last two sentences.

"What?"

"Come on, we know there's going to be drama." Lina's blank stare had been replaced by something more calculating. "They both want it. It'll make the tabloids, keep them in the news. Whatever." The woman shrugged. "You and me are just names thrown into the copy. Let's get a drink, okay?"

Griffin said nothing, blinking and staring at her like he was getting a message from God or getting Punk'd—stunned, stopped in his tracks, and speechless.

"I need to make sure Daisy is okay," he finally managed, wrestling free from her grip. "Meet you at the bar." Griffin turned and walked to where Claus and Daisy were standing…only to be intercepted by Jules.

"Hold up, it's okay for now," she said, elbow in his sternum to keep him from moving.

"It's not okay. They're going to have a fight, and everyone is watching."

"So what else is new? Did Lina go to the bar?" Jules peeked around him. "Okay, brilliant. Let's hope she gathers a bit of a crowd over there."

Griffin shook his head. "What the hell is going on here? Lina's not even French, is she?"

"What? Oh she's just not *that* French. She went to school here." Jules gave him an odd look. "Why do you ask?"

"She's just…she's just not what I expected." Hedda, Angel, Melody—all the names in recent and long-term memory were actually starlets who thought they'd be wife number three. Lina reminded him of…a stand-in. A stunt mistress, as it were. Something was definitely up.

"Go finish getting yourself some dinner, have another drink. I'll keep an eye on the craziness." Jules's voice was soothing, but Griffin still felt like everything was off. Maybe it was him, though. If he didn't want to be here before, it was tripled times ten right now.

"Right, okay." Griffin walked slowly to the now-emptied-out buffet, and gathered up an empty plate. He picked and chose, head swiveling back to Daisy and Claus's murmured conversation and then to the bar where Lina was talking to...Jules.

* * *

Griffin returned to his perch in the shade, hidden mostly from view. He picked at the fusion crap, craved a steak, and drank down another margarita. The warm evening air combined with all the tequila and weirdness had begun to take effect; he was ready for a nap or to do something stupid.

Toss-up.

Briefly he considered calling Jim again, maybe asking if he could leave this mess right now and fly back to Seattle, where things were simpler. It might be avoidance or a sense of the grass being greener, because how had he not noticed how much this merry-go-round sucked before now?

"Well, that's not true. I knew, I just didn't care," Griffin muttered to himself.

He heard footsteps approaching and peeked out from behind a frond to see who had found his hiding place.

Jules, with two bottles of Corona and a sheepish smile on her face.

"What now?" he asked.

"Nothing. I think I have some 'splainin' to do, my love."

"You know, it just hit me that perhaps this was a setup..."

"Not for you, you know that, right?"

Griffin nodded as he took the beer and moved over so Jules could park herself beside him.

"They really need to get onto the front page that badly? A fake affair *and* a fake fight?"

Jules shrugged. "It was just an innuendo thing. Or it was supposed to be. Then Claus showed up and got pissed because Daisy was actually flirting."

"He's an asshole. Lina may be a fake, but the others weren't."

"Hedda was very, very real." Jules laughed wearily as she took a sip. "My God, that was seventeen months of hell."

"I never understood why he dumped her. I was sure Daisy was destined for ex-wifehood."

Jules turned and looked him, confused and half laughing, half frowning. "What? I thought you of all people knew."

"Knew what?" Griffin felt the ground shift beneath him one more time.

"Daisy told Claus if he dumped Hedda, she'd rip up the prenup."

The cold bottle of beer almost slipped out of Griffin's hands as a shock wave went through him. "Are you serious?"

"As a heart attack, love. I can't believe she didn't tell you! It was such a big patch of drama. Even with the shredding of the prenup, I thought Claus would run off with her, but no. He and Daisy just love the drama too much. It keeps them stuck together."

That prenup was something Griffin had pushed her to get all those years ago, her cushion for when the romantic ride was over and the drama played out and Claus went for younger and hotter and whatever. It was horrifying to think she'd given it away to stop Claus from moving on. It was infuriating to know she had a chance to get away and didn't take it.

He said nothing, drinking the beer and staring at the stones under his feet.

She hadn't told him. That resonated louder than anything else.

"Griff? Love, I'm sorry. I thought for sure she told you. You're her best friend…"

Jules meant well, he was sure, but those words just stung harder.

"Yeah, I know. She probably didn't tell me so I wouldn't worry," Griffin lied. He drained his beer and left it with the other empties as he stood up. "I need to jet, Jules. Tell Daisy I'll call her later."

He heard words of protest behind him and caught a few folks trying to make conversation on the way out, but he kept walking, not slowing down until he reached the valets out front and requested his keys before realizing just how much he'd had to drink.

And the fact that Jim would be mighty pissed if he got caught driving drunk.

"Hey, listen, put my car in the garage. The bay they use for the deliveries. Just talk to Jules—it'll be fine." The head valet nodded and pocketed the keys; Griffin got out his phone and dialed the number for the studio's limo service.

He didn't want to wait out front where he could run into someone, so he started walking down the long driveway toward the road.

The car service told him twenty minutes. Griffin knocked on the window of the guard house, and they let him out with strange looks and offers of assistance, but he mumbled something about a car and kept walking.

There wasn't anywhere to actually go. The property stretched pretty far, the next closest house was at least a mile away, and Griffin had no illusions of how far he could walk (and back) before the car came.

His BlackBerry sat heavily in his pocket, beckoning him to call Jim again, but that seemed desperate bordering on lame. He didn't want to wear out his welcome. His second option was calling Daisy's voice mail and giving her a piece of his mind.

No. He needed to stew on that one a bit more. Griffin was pissed, and he could run with that—until he reached the part that it was *Daisy*, and then confusion mixed with the anger until all he wanted to do was slink away and hide.

Griffin kicked a few rocks on the road, keeping to one side so as not to end up a hood ornament on someone's Jag.

What a shitty headline that would be. DRUNK HOLLYWOOD SCREENWRITER SMASHED— LITERALLY.

"Griffin! Where the hell are you?"

He looked up and squinted toward the gate, where a slim figure was stomping toward him. He knew that stomp and sighed.

"Go back into the house, Daisy Mae."

"No! How could you leave without saying good-bye?" She reached him, swinging her shoes by the laces in his direction as she came closer.

"I'm drunk and pissed, Daisy. Go back into the house and leave me alone," he said stubbornly, stepping back from her.

"Pissed about what? I should be pissed. Claus showed up, you disappear into a corner *sulking*, and then you leave without saying good-bye. What kind of friend are you?"

And really, that was the tiny droplet that sent the reservoir overflowing.

"What kind of..." Griffin wished to God he had something to throw at this moment. "What kind of friend am I? Are you fucking delusional? Tell me something, Daisy— when were you going to tell me about the prenup?"

For a second he saw a glitter in her eyes, like she was calculating a lie, but when her head dropped, he knew he'd get the truth—or at least a version of it before she cried or threw a fit so he'd back down.

"I didn't want to tell you because I knew you'd be upset," she started, but Griffin couldn't hold his tongue.

"Smart move, because I'm furious. Goddamn it, Daisy— you had a chance to get away from him, to get out of this stupid life that sucks you dry, and you stayed? Worse, you signed away everything to stay, and then what? You whine to me about how bad it is, how much you want more out of life, and we take on this project..."

His voice trailed off, and a sudden realization almost rocked him off his feet.

"If you signed away the prenup, that means Claus owns everything."

Daisy bit her lip. "Yes."

"That means Claus technically owns the Ed Kelly project." Griffin's face went ice-cold, his heartbeats tripping over each other until they actually started to hurt his chest.

"You don't have to worry; he doesn't know about it."

"But he will, Daisy, he will. And when he does, he can do whatever he wants with it."

Claus and Bright Side were not known for their sensitive, artistic films—and Claus was not known for letting things like outbidding him for a project on the sly go by without retribution.

"He won't care." Daisy crossed her arms over her chest; he could see her pout, and it made him nauseated.

"He won't care you went behind his back, used his money, and got the hottest property in town on your own? Really? Are you new to this world, Daisy? Because I can remember about a hundred people parking cars and shampooing dogs in this town because Claus got pissed at them and made sure they didn't find work again."

"God, why are you so dramatic tonight? He's got his new girlfriend to think about, he won't care about anything but her for a good long while," she said dramatically.

"I know she's a fake."

Daisy's eyes widened in shock. "What?"

"I talked to her, I talked to Jules, and I know she's a fake. Is Claus really that worried the new *Master Fighter* movie is going to tank? Worried about market shares? Gotta keep everyone in the news? This is such bullshit."

"Jules shouldn't have told you any of this, Griffin. I didn't want to upset you..."

"You leave Jules out of this. I don't want you to even give her a hard time, Daisy—I'm totally serious here. She's been more of a friend to me tonight than you have."

Daisy went into full lip quiver, her eyes filling with tears. "That's unfair. You don't know what it's like living with him and dealing with all the bullshit, Griffin. You think you do, but you don't."

"Then you should have left when you had the chance."

She shook her head. "Right. Because there are so many opportunities for me outside of this. Producers knocking down my door, bemoaning the lack of thirtysomething actresses who do their best work naked. You have no idea."

Griffin was incredulous. "What is this? Have I been talking to your clone all these months? We've been working on this, Daisy—the Ed Kelly project, remember? But see, I've been working under the assumption we were on the same page."

"Don't worry about your project, Griffin—I won't let anything happen to it." She was humoring him, and that just set him off further. He felt completely used—by the last person he could ever imagine doing this to him.

Headlights swung over them as a black sedan waited at the gate twenty feet away; Griffin thanked the gods for perfect timing and began walking toward the car, ignoring Daisy entirely.

"Griffin!" Daisy called after him.

He kept walking.

Chapter Seventeen

Jim changed the sheets and brought the laundry downstairs to put the last load in before bed. He felt tired but accomplished, a good feeling to take between the covers with him. There was even another day of his weekend off to enjoy…although that was puzzling him a bit. What to do with a Sunday when you had no chores, no work, and no company.

He considered calling someone in the Cabal, but he knew Terry and Mimi had "plans," Heather and Nick were doing wedding stuff, and well, he hadn't had much luck in working up the courage to spend time with Ben and Liddy. While his best friend had no idea, Jim still churned with guilt over his crush, half nursing his idolized version of Ben and half wondering what in the hell he had been thinking.

It was embarrassing. No one knew except Matt in New York, but it was still cringeworthy.

So that left him alone for Sunday.

As he measured detergent into the machine, a thought crossed his mind, a wild, wild thought about calling Griffin, but he chased that away.

He closed the machine, turned to go into the kitchen for something to eat before bed, and the phone rang.

55555

555555555555

"Shit," he muttered. A ringing phone at midnight meant work for a homicide detective. He was surprised they called his landline, but he grabbed the receiver and barked, "Shea."

"Uhhhh…Drake?"

"Griffin?"

"Jim?"

Jim laughed. "Yeah, it's me—sorry for that. I thought it was work."

"So I'm guessing right and you were awake?"

"Yeah." Jim paused. Something sounded off. "You okay?"

"Yeah. No. No, not really. Hey, can I ask for a favor?"

"Sure."

"If I showed up on your doorstep tomorrow, could I hang out and write on your sofa? I swear I'll be quiet and really clean."

They'd talked hours before about Griffin coming back, but this didn't sound like a request for a long date. It sounded like a place to hide out for a while.

"You on the run from the law, son?"

"No. Just avoiding everyone I know for a bit. That cool?"

"Sure. You need me to pick you up at the airport?"

"My flight gets in at one o'clock."

"You got a gate?"

"You got a pen?"

* * *

Later, in bed, Jim stretched out and watched the ceiling fan above him. He wasn't at all disappointed about Griffin coming back so quickly, though he was concerned about the tone of his voice. Griffin wouldn't say what was wrong, promised it wasn't too bad, and then quickly got off the phone.

He considered things that might be wrong and came up with nothing. He didn't know the other man well enough to guess and didn't have enough experience with "relationships" to venture a hypothesis.

He considered things to do to cheer Griffin up and came up with grilling steaks and sex.

He hoped that was at least a good start.

But Jim clearly needed a little assistance.

* * *

"You're calling me at nine on a Sunday to ask for relationship advice?" Matt Haight sounded deeply amused. "Hang on, lemme get my coffee and a tape recorder."

"Unfunny."

"Hilarious, actually."

Jim heard noise in the background—kids' voices, the television. Matt calling that he was on the phone and please keep it down, and then a door closing.

"All right. I made it to relative safety and quiet, but I gotta warn you, we have a Little League game at eleven."

"This isn't going to take that long." Jim was exasperated and embarrassed and feeling silly. "I just have a question."

"Go. Wait, lemme get comfortable… Okay, hit me."

"I wish I could."

"Har, har. So is this movie-related?"

"No, and sorta. I'm, uh—I think I'm dating the guy who's writing the movie."

"You think?"

"I am." Jim looked around the living room to make sure no one had materialized to overhear.

"And how are things going?" Matt was clearly delighted by this news.

"Good, pretty good. I like him. He's a good guy to hang out with."

"Wow, that's some gush for you."

"So we haven't known each other long, and he's coming to stay with me again…"

"Again?"

"Yes, again."

"Hmmmm."

"You're an ass."

"Get to the problem, Detective, or else I'll have to brush off my interrogation skills."

"He called last night, and he seemed really down."

"Okay. Did you ask him what was wrong?"

"No, I asked him if he liked cats—of course I asked. He doesn't want to talk about it."

"Uhhhh-huh. So we've established he's a typical man. Proceed."

"He's flying in today, and I just wasn't sure what I should do."

"Pick him up at the airport."

"Matt…"

"No, seriously." Matt laughed. "Pick him up, take him to eat, be a buddy. Then get him into bed. If he wants to tell you, he will. If not, at least you'll be showing him you care how he's feeling."

Interesting—that was pretty much what Jim thought. Good first instincts, at least.

"That's it?"

"Or you can strap him to a chair and interrogate his ass. I know you know how to do that."

"Awww. You sound like you miss it."

"I don't have to miss it. Katie is attracting miscreants like mosquitoes. I'm considering the purchase of a taser."

"That's very domestic in a weird sort of way."

* * *

Matt and Jim shot the shit for a little bit longer; Matt pushed for details about Griffin and promised to look him up online. He threw in a sincere good luck at the end of their conversation, and Jim was thankful his stupid smile was unseen by the other man. It seemed ridiculous for a forty-five-year-old man to be this confused over how to handle serious dating.

After he hung up, Jim felt a little bit steadier. He changed into jeans and a T-shirt, took some steaks out to defrost. The apartment all but gleamed in the sunlight through the tall windows—showroom perfect but a bit...stiff.

All the art and pictures belonged to Ben, and they'd left when he moved out. Jim had repainted but never replaced anything else, so now he had perfect, gleaming beige walls and that was it.

Even a picture of dogs playing poker would liven up the joint.

He faithfully wrote down *buy stuff for walls* on his perpetual to-do list on the fridge, then grabbed his keys. There was time to kill before he met Griffin's flight, but Jim was too anxious to stay inside another second.

* * *

Jim made it through half of *Angels & Demons*— purchased at a magazine stand along with an iced tea— waiting for Griffin's plane. It was engrossing enough to keep him from checking the arrival screen forty times a minute for an entire hour, which made it worth every penny.

When the flight from Los Angeles was announced, Jim gathered up his book, sticking it under his arm as he approached the arrival gate. He tried to look casual, which made him feel distinctly *un*casual, crossing and uncrossing his arms until it looked like he had a serious tic.

Thankfully Griffin's head appeared in the departing crowd, and Jim relaxed enough to smile and give a little wave.

Griffin seemed lost in his thoughts and didn't notice Jim until he reached the end of the ramp. When he saw him, a grin appeared, making Jim feel like approximately five million bucks.

"Hey," he said, hauling a small suitcase behind him, another bag over his shoulder.

"Hey, that's all you got, or do we have to go to luggage claim?"

"No, this is it." Griffin's smile wavered slightly. "Thanks for picking me up, by the way."

"My pleasure. Actually I was trying to figure what to do today, and your call was perfectly timed."

"Well, I will do my best to be entertaining."

Jim shrugged. "I'm pretty easy to please. I'm just glad you're here."

That seemed to break Griffin's smile down further, so Jim brazenly reached down and took his hand. He couldn't work up the balls to actually kiss the man, so he hoped that would be enough—for now.

"I'm, uh—thanks, Jim. I kinda needed to hear that." Griffin laughed nervously. "Can we get going? I haven't slept yet, and I'm about to face-plant on this lovely carpet right here."

"Yeah, come on." Jim didn't even ask; he just grabbed the handle of the rolling suitcase and urged Griffin toward the escalator.

* * *

Griffin stayed quiet through the trip back to the loft, and Jim didn't push. He understood silence better than most people, and he recognized Griffin was processing; chatter wouldn't do anything but piss him off at this point.

Jim parked and grabbed both bags this time; Griffin murmured, "Thank you," and followed him upstairs with ever-dragging legs. They just about made it into the loft before Griffin's eyes were closed, even as his body kept moving under Jim's urging.

"Upstairs," he said, leaving the luggage near the door. "Just keep going; I'm right behind you."

Griffin got up the stairs and even got his shoes off before crawling under the covers; he mumbled something like "I missed you, bed" before burying his face in the pillow and shutting off like a light switch had been flicked.

Jim chuckled as he put Griffin's shoes under the bed. He headed back down to the kitchen to get their lunch/dinner started and leave Griffin to his nap.

The balcony was made for days like this: slightly overcast as usual, but warm and breezy. Jim set up the grill and sat down with the rest of his novel, passing a few hours of quiet anticipation.

"Thanks, I needed that," Griffin's gravelly voice said, and Jim startled awake from a postbook nap. "Sorry."

"No, no. Just a doze." Jim turned in his chair with a smile. Griffin looked a lot less hangdog, his hair crazy in every possible direction. "You need something to drink?"

"Nursing a hangover, so, uh—anything that isn't alcoholic." Griffin laughed, settling into the second Adirondack chair.

"I have iced tea."

"That works."

Jim brought out two glasses and the plate of steaks, plus two foil-wrapped potatoes. Griffin gave him a whistle as he reappeared, relieving him of the drinks.

"Wow. When you said you were going to cook for me, I had no idea it involved the grilling of meat."

"It's either this or spaghetti."

"That's like…two more things than I can make."

"I thought your dad was a feminist. Didn't he teach you to cook?"

"Nah, that's his domain. I think he thinks it's a great secret he's keeping, lest he be declared obsolete." Griffin yawned and drank the iced tea, stretching out in a pocket of sun like a contented cat.

"Your dad is an interesting character."

"Oh, that's a really great way to put it." Griffin cracked open one eye in Jim's direction. "You'd like him, I think. He's pretty no-nonsense."

"I'm no-nonsense?"

"Dude, nonsense is actually afraid of you, that's how no-nonsense you are."

Jim shook his head as he put the steaks and potatoes on the grill.

"What about your dad? I saw—well, I read your mom passed away when you were really young," Griffin said apologetically.

"I was two. I really don't remember her at all." Jim shrugged. His mother was a stranger in photographs, so missing her never made sense to him. It was easier to miss having a father when one lived in the house with you but didn't seem to give a shit. "My brother was seven, so he has more memories of her."

"Are you close?"

"To my father or my brother? The answer's the same for both—we barely speak. Once a year we get together to visit my father at the home he's in, and that's about it."

"That sucks." Griffin lost his relaxed pose, leaning forward to angle his body toward Jim, to give him his attention. "I'm not super close to my sisters, but we all talk and see each other as much as we can."

"How many sisters did you have again?"

"Eight. All older."

"Eight?" Jim whistled.

Griffin shrugged. "It's what you do where I'm from. Winters are long. Plus there are two sets of twins, so that adds up."

"Eight sisters, and you're the youngest? That must've been fun." Jim settled down in the chair next to Griffin, glad to have changed the subject from his family. It wasn't something he liked revisiting.

"Actually, it was. I didn't have to suffer through hand-me-downs, my sisters beat up anyone who got in my face, and the neighborhood kids let me play ball with them on the off chance they would come watch."

Jim laughed. "Well, there's a bright side, then."

"After my mom died, they were all my moms. Plus my dad was my mom. Basically I go broke every Mother's Day."

"How…" Jim stopped. "Never mind, sorry."

"How old was I? Hey, it's okay; I asked you stuff." Griffin shrugged. "She died when I was six. Aneurysm. One minute, hanging out laundry. Next minute, gone." He snapped his fingers. "A really good reminder of how life changes in an instant, you know?"

Jim remembered Della Kelly's face the seconds before she collapsed, and nodded.

"You have to live your life and not count on things being there tomorrow or the next day." Griffin looked off into the distance, then shook his head. "Sorry—you see reminders of that every single day. No need for me to wax philosophically like a talking fortune cookie."

"No, no. You're right." Jim took a sip of iced tea. "I forget that sometimes, even with my line of work. I get caught up on the bad stuff, feeling hopeless and helpless and forgetting that for all the shit I see, there's gotta be good stuff going on somewhere."

"Man, you need a vacation."

"Probably. But I won't take one."

"At least you're honest." Griffin paused. "I guess when you love what you do that much, it's hard to walk away."

Jim started to agree, then stopped, twisting thoughts around in his head. Loved his job? Did he?

"I don't know if it's love…"

"Oh, come on, Jim—it's not a person; it's your career. You can commit a little," Griffin teased.

"No, I mean—I joined the army to piss off my father. It wasn't what I wanted, but I was good at aspects of it. So when I got out, I thought—what else can I do that's like the military? And I came up with police work…which also had the benefit of pissing my father off."

Jim kicked one of Griffin's outstretched legs. "Stop making that face."

"I'm just a little surprised, man—I guess I had this vision of you as heroic savior guy."

"Nah. I'm a workaholic, I like details, I like a neatly tied bow on the end of everything. It works out."

"Wouldn't you rather do something you love?"

"I don't really love anything."

"That's not true! You love, uh…cleaning."

"So I should chuck the police thing and become a janitor?"

"If you love it, why not?"

Jim rolled his eyes and headed for the grill.

"No, wait—you could open one of those cleaning companies where they clean up crime scenes…"

"Yeah, no." Jim turned the steaks over and poked the potatoes a few times.

"How about consultant work? Come to Hollywood, get a job on a television show as a consultant, and sit by the pool answering questions about bullet holes."

"I might not be in love with police work, but I am good at it. I'm staying put. No offense."

"Hmph."

"So I'm guessing you love what you do? Even though you're, uh—what did you call it? A Twinkie?"

Griffin rolled out of the chair and walked around the balcony. "Yeah, well—my job is artificial cake with a gooey filling, but I never wanted to be anything but a writer. Ever."

"Huh."

"Is that surprising?"

"Guess not. Writing doesn't seem like something you do without some sort of passion behind it."

"That's true." Jim's words seemed to trigger something in Griffin; he walked around the balcony again, that look of processing back on his face. "I do have a passion for it—I think I just forgot to fire it up for a while."

"But Ed's story—that's firing you up again?"

Griffin looked at Jim, a little surprise on his face, but he nodded slowly. "Yeah. I think Ed's story is exactly what I need, maybe for reasons I didn't even think of." He smiled. "Thanks."

"For what?"

Griffin walked over close and leaned into Jim's personal space, or at least the space not taken up by the grill. "For picking me up at the airport, for making me dinner, and for helping me get my head out of my ass."

Jim smirked as their lips met; he had a really awesome double entendre to throw on that comment but accepted being halted by the sweet curl of Griffin's tongue against his.

* * *

This time they ate first and fucked later, Jim gripping the headboard with white knuckles as Griffin worked himself into a foul-mouthed frenzy. Every time he promised to fuck Jim into next week—and punctuated it with a fierce snap of his hips—Jim smiled through the moans and lip-biting pain.

Everything was going according to his "plan," including the side benefit of an orgasm that nearly shook him over the edge of the sleeping loft to the ground below.

"What a way to go." He wheezed into the pillow, as Griffin pumped through his own release with an unhurried pace.

"Whu?"

"Nothin'."

Chapter Eighteen

Griffin got up quietly, leaving Jim sleeping peacefully and drooling on his pillow. The clock said 5:38, and the movement of the clouds outside said maybe some rain very shortly.

He walked downstairs without bothering with clothes. There was something on his mind, something he had to do right now before he lost his nerve.

The MacBook was set up on the counter, his BlackBerry right beside it. He made the transfer through his bank account first, moving the money to his checking account with an audible gulp. It represented a lot of his savings. It was a gamble. But it would give him some peace of mind…

The next thing he pulled up was a contract template, filling in the blanks rapidly as he gained some momentum with every word. Daisy wanted to stay in the crazy? Fine. He wasn't going to. He wasn't waiting for her to get tired of the never-ending drama.

The contract and electronic check were double-checked, triple-checked—Griffin said a nondenominational prayer—and forwarded the whole thing to Daisy's private e-mail address.

A perfectly legitimate offer for the rights to Ed Kelly's story.

* * *

"Everything okay?" Jim asked as he walked back up the stairs, lost in thought.

"Shit—did I wake you?" Griffin climbed into bed, sprawling over Jim's sleep-warm body like he belonged there.

"Nah. Not used to napping in the middle of the day."

"I wore you out, admit it." Griffin rubbed his hands over Jim's stomach and chest, eager to move his thoughts from the e-mail he had just sent and onto things less earth-shattering but much more fun. Like sex with Jim.

"I admit no such thing." Jim returned the favor, stroking his hand straight down to grip Griffin's cock.

"Touché."

Griffin rolled onto his back, taking Jim's hand with him. Followed by Jim's mouth, which joined his hand a few moments later.

He closed his eyes and spread his legs, all eager and unashamed as Jim chuckled, the vibrations dancing through Griffin's body.

"That feels good. Gonna tell you jokes while you blow me."

Jim didn't seem to agree with that option; he doubled his efforts from "lazy suck" to "vacuum cleaner," and Griffin's back arched and his hands gripped the sheets. There was no slacking off, no slowing down, no teasing. Griffin couldn't get another word out, just puffs of breath and moans trickling out as Jim worked his shaft up and down like he had a point to prove.

Like—Jim gives outstanding blowjobs, and frankly, Griffin should feel ashamed of his subpar ones.

"Slow...down," Griffin finally ground out, but it was too late because Jim had a rhythm down that gave him no chance to do anything but curse Jim's parentage and spill down his throat.

* * *

"Admit it, I wore you out..." Jim whistled a cheerful tune next to him, and Griffin would have laughed if he had any oxygen left in his lungs.

He thumped him in the side instead.

Jim laughed. "You want anything?"

"Air?"

"Wuss."

Jim threw back the covers and headed downstairs; Griffin admired the view until it was gone.

"Water!" he yelled.

"Right," Jim yelled back.

Griffin rolled around on the giant bed like a kid. He had a buzz of energy growing under his skin. He wanted to *do* something (besides Jim), and then he wanted to take his laptop onto Jim's balcony and write something fabulous.

"We should do something," Griffin said as Jim came back up the stairs.

"We just did."

"Something else."

Jim drank some of the bottled water and handed it to Griffin. "I got nothing."

"Come on, man, help me out here. Call your friends or something."

It was clearly on Jim's mind to say no, but Griffin was pleasantly surprised when Jim capitulated with only the smallest sigh.

"Okay, but I warned you in advance about the yenta factor."

"Duly noted."

Jim mumbled a few things under his breath and picked up his cell; he dialed a number, then mock glared at Griffin.

"Hey, Terry? Jim. How's it going? So, you and Mimi up for some dinner?" He paused. "No, I didn't hit my head. No, this isn't a code because I'm being held hostage."

Griffin almost rolled off the bed laughing.

"Six thirty? You sure? Okay. We'll meet you at the diner." He hung up and hmphed.

"Happy?"

"Yeah." Griffin wiped the tears of mirth out of his eyes and got out of bed, stalking Jim with a predatory glare. "You made dinner plans for me. I'm touched."

"Terry said double date," Jim despaired. "I could hear Mimi giggling in the background. It's going to be a nightmare."

"It's going to be awesome."

* * *

The diner looked like it fell out of a set from 1965, but the menu was pure Pacific Northwest. Fish, fourteen kinds of coffee, and vegan food. Perfect for the foursome seated in a booth near the back.

There were introductions and smiles and then some goofy grins. Mimi and Terry Oh were the epitome of a cute couple; they clearly each believed the other hung the moon, and their shirts kinda matched. They looked at Jim with affection and Griffin with complete amazement.

Griffin liked them immediately.

"You're real," Mimi announced as they opened their menus.

"Uh…yes I am," Griffin said. Jim rolled his eyes.

"This is a first. I hope you know that."

"The first…real guy Jim has brought out to meet anyone?" he finished.

"It's not like I brought fake ones," Jim muttered. "Just for that, I'm getting steak."

"We had steak for lunch."

"Yes, dear."

Mimi tittered with delight.

The waitress saved them from further comic stylings by taking their orders; half the table ordered red meat, and the other half ordered salads.

"Can I get a slice of chocolate cake first?" Mimi asked as she handed over her menu. Terry didn't comment, but Griffin picked up the faint blush on his cheeks.

"Dessert first, that's an excellent way to live," he commented with a smile, hoping to find and get on her good side. Because whether or not Jim articulated it, clearly his friends were important to him. And it was kind of amazing that he was here as well.

"I'm, uh…" Mimi looked at Terry, who shrugged, then nodded. "Actually, we have some news…"

Griffin could guess what it was in a second, but Jim was still looking a little confused.

"We're going to have a baby," Terry said to his partner, drawing out the words with exaggeration.

"Oh!" Jim said. He looked at Griffin, then at Terry, a huge smile dawning. "Son of a gun, congratulations."

There were handshakes and standing and shuffling around so Jim could give Mimi a hug. Griffin didn't know anyone well enough for more than a handshake, but Mimi didn't seem to care—she walked over and gave him a squeeze.

"I can't believe Jim has a boyfriend," she squeaked quietly, and Griffin was truly touched by how delighted she was.

It was sweet, and yet he wanted to correct her even as he didn't.

Boyfriend?

Too soon. Way too soon. He didn't want this to be a "Griffin jumps too soon" repeat.

"You don't have a wife, do you?" he whispered in Jim's ear as they sat down.

"Uh, no." Jim looked at him strangely, then continued his conversation with Terry. They tried to talk work briefly, but Mimi elbowed her husband and the topic switched to sports.

Tremendously domestic, absolutely a double date. Jokes and chatter and at no point until the check came did anyone mention the movie.

And it wasn't even Griffin.

"So you really going to interview me and the others about the Kelly case?" Terry asked, clearly a bit more excited than Jim was about the whole thing.

"Yeah, actually. You and Nick and Heather."

Terry shook his head. "It's weird. That was my first big case. When it started, I barely knew Jim, and now here we are…"

"However you're going to finish that sentence—stop," Jim said drily, picking up the check and waving away protests.

"I was going to say 'and now we're good friends.'" Terry all but fluttered his eyelashes to convey the sincerity of his words. Jim threw a napkin at him.

"So you know, James Oh—great name," he threw out.

"It's already on the list!" Mimi laughed as they walked outside.

"All right, Griffin, great to meet you." Terry shook his hand heartily. "Can't wait to sit down with you about the screenplay."

"He's a frustrated actor." Mimi sighed as she gave Griffin a wink. "Come to dinner next Friday, okay? I won't take no for an answer."

"Mimi…"

"James! No arguments. This one is real, and I really like him. Bring beer," she added as she took Terry's arm and they sauntered away.

Griffin whistled. "Yentas for the win."

"Told you."

* * *

Back at the loft, Griffin grabbed his laptop while Jim suggested a nap—an actual nap and not something dirty. Griffin gave him a kiss and sent him upstairs; he had ideas swirling in his head and wanted to spend some time writing.

He also wanted to check his e-mail for a response from Daisy.

There was nothing.

Griffin simmered for a few moments. Clearly this was a temper tantrum and he had to wait it out. Of course, handling this the way he always did could be a mistake, since he'd been suffering under the delusion that they were in this together.

The depth of the betrayal was hitting him bit by bit.

Once upon a time, he'd become the best friend and constant companion of the most beautiful and actually talented girl in arts camp. It elevated his status with counselors and campers alike.

When Daisy got asked back the next three years, so did he. Full scholarship.

When she attracted Claus's eye during a showcase in Manhattan, Griffin went with her to Hollywood, first as friend, then as Claus's pet screenwriter. As her star rose, so did his.

His entire career was entwined with hers; his entire life had focused on Daisy for almost two decades.

He was kind of an idiot.

Chapter Nineteen

"I'm only letting you get away with the teasing because your wife is pregnant," Jim said as Terry weaved his car through midday traffic.

"That makes no sense."

"Yes it does. Make a left."

There were on their way to a crime scene, and Terry was passing the time spent behind slow-moving drivers by asking Jim pointed questions about Griffin. As he had for the last three days.

"He's a nice guy."

"He is."

"Smart, I'm guessing."

"Very."

"You seem like you two are having fun."

"We are, thanks for asking."

Terry hmmmmed and drove through back streets until they finally arrived at the cordoned-off area. A uniform met them at the corner, his face white and drawn.

"Rookie," Terry muttered as he and Jim pulled out plastic gloves and snapped them on.

"That was you in very recent memory, partner."

"I told you—I had the flu."

"For six months?"

* * *

"We still going to Ed's tonight?" Griffin asked. Jim could hear busy sounds through the phone. Maybe the dock. Griffin had made noises before Jim left that morning about getting out, getting some writing done.

"I'm hoping. Depends on how early I get out of here." Jim peeled the paper off a granola bar as Terry finished up with some of the victim's neighbors. "Let me rephrase that—we're probably leaving really early in the morning, and can you drive the truck?"

"It's been a while since I drove a tank, but sure."

"Good. Because chances are I'll be unconscious."

"Then I have control of the radio? Exxxxcellent."

"My radio is broken. It only picks up classic rock."

Griffin snorted. "Go back to work. I'll see you…whenever."

"Now there's a plan. Later."

Terry walked over while Jim was chewing.

"How's the boyfriend?"

Jim gave him the finger.

"I'm not teasing, you know. Mimi and I discussed it—he's your boyfriend."

"We're dating. That's it."

"He's practically living with you. You introduced him to me and Mimi." Terry ticked off each thing on a finger. "Face it, Jim—he's your boyfriend."

Jim scowled. "Teasing amnesty over. Let's get back to the station."

"Boyfriend."

"Shut up."

* * *

Jim didn't see Griffin again until four a.m. when he staggered upstairs and into bed next to the other man. Actually he only saw the parts of Griffin not wrapped up in the sheets as he snored on, even as Jim accidentally kicked over the garbage can in the dark.

Five hours later the alarm buzzed, and Jim lifted his fuzzy head off the pillow to the smell of coffee and something cinnamony sweet.

"I know it's only two hours, but we gotta get up there," Griffin called from down below. "Shower first; then you get caffeine. *Then* you get a cinnamon roll."

Jim muttered something even he didn't understand as he rolled from the bed.

"You can sleep in the car!"

"Why are you so chipper?" Jim mumbled as he tripped down the stairs.

"Less chipper, more caffeinated." Griffin had already dressed in khaki shorts and a black Grateful Dead T-shirt. He was pouring coffee into a thermos and smiled. "Possibly sugared up too."

"God, that was a long day."

"And night and part of a morning." Griffin stopped his kitchen activities and met Jim near the bottom of the stairs for a kiss. "You smell like fish tacos."

"You don't want to know why."

"Yeah, I really don't."

* * *

Two and a half hours later, Griffin was pulling the truck—very carefully—into Ed's driveway.

"I'm never driving this tank again."

"Don't speak ill of the beast."

Ed met them at the door, all smiles as he opened the screen door.

"Good mornin', gentlemen," he called as they approached.

Jim tried not to react to the way Ed looked; it had only been a few weeks, but clearly he'd lost a significant amount of weight. The gauntness, the grayness of his skin—there wasn't any way Griffin was going to miss that.

"Hey, Ed, sorry we're late. Late night on a case," Jim said quickly, up the stairs and in the house in a split second. He wanted Ed to go sit down as soon as possible.

"Don't apologize, Jim, I understand. Hello, Mr. Drake." Ed smiled as he extended his hand.

"Griffin, please," Griffin said quietly, and Jim knew without turning around that Griffin knew something was very wrong.

"Griffin. Come on in. I have coffee on."

They sat down at the dining room table, and Jim insisted on playing host. He avoided Griffin's face, lest it all come tumbling out.

"How's the movie comin'?" Ed asked Griffin.

"Pretty good, actually. Apparently Seattle is the answer to my writer's block."

"You got a place there now?"

"Actually, he's staying with me," Jim said quickly. Ed's smile was expansive.

"Ohhhh, that's nice to hear." Ed was more subtle than Terry or Mimi, but Jim ducked his head regardless. The older man sounded entirely too amused.

"Jim's a good host," Griffin offered, and that didn't really help. Jim shoved a cookie in his mouth. "So I thought if you didn't mind, or it wouldn't be too difficult..."

Ed held up one hand. "Son, I understand you'll be askin' me some tough questions. Knew that when I said yes. I thought we could go through some pictures and things I have saved...maybe it'll help you some, and you can ask me whatever you need to know."

"Thank you," Griffin said sincerely. "And if you need to stop, just say so."

"Fair enough."

* * *

Jim knew the stories well enough; he didn't stick to his seat on the sofa for long after Ed's storytelling began. He knew Ed met Della at a USO dance. He knew Ed was 4-F because of his flat feet and bad eyes. He knew Della's family thought she could do better.

They eloped to Niagara Falls when Della turned eighteen. Ed was twenty. They tried for years to have a baby, but it took fifteen years of marriage before Carmen came along. She was a much desired, much loved only child, and the Kellys were delighted.

So maybe all those years made them a little overprotective. Maybe the long hours worked by Ed—to make sure there was enough money for everything—took their toll on Della and Carmen, who seemed to have polar-opposite personalities. Whatever the case, Carmen started down the typical teenager path in high school—the wrong friends, the wrong parties, the wrong attitude.

Then she disappeared.

They called the police, but runaway seventeen-year-olds in this part of the country were a dime a dozen. Ed and Della had no idea where she might have gone. When the first tattered postcard arrived, they were almost killed with relief.

She was in Seattle. She was fine. She was making her own way. Don't worry.

But worrying was all they had now. Della went to church every day and prayed. Ed worked hard and spent his nights driving down to Seattle to look for her—futile, of course, in a big city, but he had to do something.

Then the call they were dreading came.

Carmen was dead, her body found in a parking lot, strangled. In a neighborhood known for running rampant with prostitutes and drug dealers.

The implication was clear—nothing much could be done, would be done. So sorry for your loss.

"I never said that," Jim called from the kitchen where he was making lunch.

"I know, son, I know. Just a feelin' I got," Ed called back and winked at Griffin.

"So I got mad. And I'm not really a fella who gets mad, but oh boy, I was pissed. So instead of drivin' around to find Carmen now, I drove down to Seattle and asked to speak to the detective in charge of Carmen's case."

"I'd like to point out in advance it was eight at night when this happened..." Jim brought in a tray of sandwiches and iced tea.

"Jim wasn't exactly thrilled to meet me." Ed smiled. "But he said, 'Let's go sit and talk,' and we did. I told him about Carmen and about me and Della and how we knew Carmen wasn't leading a perfect life, but that didn't mean whoever killed her deserved to get away."

He sighed then and Jim fidgeted. He hated this part of the story, because he ultimately failed Ed and Della and Carmen—Tripp Ingersoll was a free man.

"I know the rest," Griffin said quietly. "If you don't want to keep going."

Ed nodded and reached for something to drink, bypassing the sandwiches. "Jim bore the rest of the burden.

He worked so hard on Carmen's case, more hours than I'm sure anyone knows about."

"It's my job," Jim interjected.

Ed gave him a hand wave to dismiss that.

"Then after the trial and Della's passing—well, he's taken very good care of me."

"Enough, please. This movie isn't about me."

"Maybe it should be," Griffin said, and Jim gave him a glare. But then he winked, and Jim knew he was being ribbed.

"Jim, the action-hero cop with a heart—maybe even a television program. I'd watch that," Ed teased.

Jim took his sandwich and iced tea and stalked back into the kitchen.

Laughter followed him, and he sat down at the table with a smile on his face.

* * *

Ed fell asleep at some point in the afternoon. Jim was used to it, but Griffin clearly was not. Jim took the other man by the arm and led him outside for a quiet conversation.

He didn't want to betray Ed's trust, but...

"What's wrong with him?" Griffin asked as they sat on the front steps, side by side, thigh to thigh.

"Listen, you have to swear not to tell anyone—not even Daisy."

"I promise, Jim, honestly. Just...what's wrong with him? He's sick, that much I can tell."

"Pancreatic cancer." Jim sighed deeply. "He hasn't got that much time left. To be honest, he won't be around long enough to see your movie get made." It hurt to be honest, but saying the words aloud was almost a relief to Jim. He'd been carrying this secret around for so long with no respite.

"Shit." Griffin folded his arms and laid his chin down. "Why is he doing this movie, then? If he's not even going to be around?"

"Money, I guess. I don't really know. There's no one to leave anything to, and I'm handling all the legal stuff after he's gone."

"Do you think…" Griffin looked at him sideways. "Maybe he's going to leave the money to you."

That startled Jim, and he shook his head. "I have more money than I know what to do with."

"Does Ed know you're a trust-fund baby? Or does he think you're a really hardworking cop who only has his pension waiting for him?"

They were good questions; Jim pondered them as he watched a few birds pecking the lawn for food. They hadn't ever discussed Jim's monetary situation, and without a search of public records, it was doubtful Ed would find out how much money his grandfather left him when he died.

"Well, fuck," Jim muttered.

"Yeah, so…" Griffin's voice trailed off. "Listen, Jim, maybe this movie isn't such a good idea, you know?"

"It's what Ed wants, and I'm going to comply with his wishes. If the money is coming to me, then I'll do what you suggested in that first meeting…a community garden, a scholarship. All the money will go to projects in the Kellys' name."

"That's very nice of you. I know how much you hate this Hollywood stuff."

Jim shrugged. "Hollywood's still weird, but I'm glad I met you out of the deal."

Griffin smiled and Jim followed suit. It was hard to resist Griffin in his natural tousled state with those glasses and impossible-to-entirely-control hair.

"You liiiike me," Griffin teased.

Jim gave him a shove.

"Well, you like me." He coughed.

"Yeah, I do."

* * *

Ed woke up a few minutes later and joined them outside. Jim got up to pace, leaving the other two men the steps.

There was some general chitchat, with Ed declaring it was Griffin's turn to spill out his family life.

Griffin had good stories of his hometown and his slightly unconventional family. He talked about his father a great deal, Jim listening with half an ear as Griffin recounted Bill Drake's single parenting of nine closely spaced children.

"We might have gotten a reality show out of it, but alas, wrong decade," Griffin said drily, and Ed laughed.

"Your dad must be proud of you," Ed said.

Griffin nodded. "He is. I'm sort of an alien in my family, but he's proud. Encouraging. I kinda miss him, to be honest."

"You should go see him soon," Ed advised, coughing into his hand a bit. "Take Jim."

Griffin and Jim blushed in tandem, which Ed found hilarious.

"I wish I had a camera right now." He snickered.

* * *

They stayed a little longer, but Ed was clearly tiring again. Jim and Griffin got into the truck and waved at the slender figure in the driveway.

Silence reigned for most of the ride back into Seattle.

"Why do you think Tripp Ingersoll was found not guilty?" Griffin asked suddenly.

Jim's hand vibrated on the wheel.

"The jury didn't want to believe a kid with that much going for him would throw it away by strangling a hooker in a parking lot."

"Carmen was just a kid, though…"

"And she had already wasted her life. Drugs, hooking, misdemeanor crime. They wrote her off."

Jim's voice was surprisingly calm. He hadn't discussed the case much since the verdict.

"There was evidence."

"No smoking gun. He admitted having sex with her that night, so that explained the forensics. He said he left her in the parking lot. She was alive. Someone else must've come along and done it…"

"That's…"

"Possible in that neighborhood, or at least in the minds of the jury."

Griffin hmphed loudly and kicked the dash.

"I know." Jim switched lanes, slowing down as the traffic began to build. "Believe me. I hated that jury for a long time. But they did their best."

"You're being too nice."

"I thought I was no-nonsense."

"Apparently you're also a solid-gold Boy Scout." There was affection in Griffin's voice, and Jim looked over to meet his gaze for a moment.

"I'm just a guy."

"Cute guy."

"Stop."

"You're extra cute when you blush."

"I'm leaving you on the side of the road in five seconds if you don't cut that out."

Griffin laughed and played with the radio for the rest of the ride to the loft.

Chapter Twenty

When there was no word from Daisy by the end of the week, Griffin kissed Jim good-bye, grabbed his wallet, and hopped a flight back to Los Angeles. He figured he'd be back in time for a late dinner with Jim, and he would be none the wiser.

But enough was enough.

Griffin took a car over to Bright Side's studio, double-checking at the gate that Claus was, indeed, on-site today.

"Good morning, Dawn! I need to see Claus," he said as he breezed into the executive offices. The blonde bombshell behind the desk looked up and then down again.

"He's in a meeting," she said, bored and disinterested.

"Tough. It's an emergency."

"Come back later." She gave him a glare over the desk. "Seriously, Griffin, come back later. Like…two hours. You don't want to interrupt him right now."

Dawn throwing him a bone was a surprise; Griffin nodded and slid his sunglasses back on. "I'm going to the commissary and charging something expensive to the account. See you in two hours."

He sauntered out before she changed her benevolence.

Griffin ate a tuna sandwich and wandered around the studios for a while. He had some friends here and there to shoot the shit with. There was a shoot going on—apparently Nico had been rehired, because Lina was shooting her debut on soundstage two.

He hung out for a bit watching. Lina was untalented but absolutely gorgeous; no doubt the camera loved her. She followed the director's comments faithfully, her face set and serious with each take.

Maybe she had a future as the next Daisy. Griffin wanted to warn her it wasn't all it was cracked up to be.

He left instead. No one believed you when you gave advice like that. Everyone thought they were different, special. It wouldn't happen to *them*.

Just like Griffin believed it wouldn't happen to *him*. He wouldn't be jerked around or betrayed. He could count on his friends.

He could count on squat.

Back in Claus's office, Dawn waved him into the inner sanctuary.

It was decorated like a safari hunter's wet dream, right down to the heads on the wall. Griffin always thought he put giant horned heads up there because human ones would be illegal. But Claus would if he could.

"What do you want?"

"Nice to see you too, Claus." Griffin sat down in one of the plush leather chairs across the room. "I need to talk to you about something."

"Talk fast—I have meetings with actual important people in fifteen minutes." Claus hadn't even looked up from his computer since Griffin walked in.

"The Ed Kelly project."

Claus looked up.

"What about it?"

"So you know."

Claus made a sputtering, gasping sound that Griffin recognized as his attempt at a chuckle.

"Of course I know. Daisy's business is my business. Why you two thought you could hide it from me, I don't know."

"We're just two kooky kids on an adventure." Griffin leaned forward, twirling his sunglasses. "I want to buy the project from you."

"I own it? Oh yes, I do. Because my wife lost everything when she signed away the prenup." Claus smirked.

"How much?"

"Two million."

"Claus, give me a break, okay? You know I don't have that kind of money."

"Then you can't have it." Claus shrugged. "I've actually procured the services of a second screenwriter to work on the story."

Griffin's jaw snapped shut. "It's my project, Claus. I've already done the interviews and the research…"

"You haven't talked to everyone."

"What are you talking about?"

"Come back today at four. I'll have a great person for you to talk to about the Ed Kelly case."

"Claus…"

"Do you want to write this or not?" All business now, Claus pressed the Intercom button and Dawn's voice came through.

"Dawn, confirm my appointment at four and add Mr. Drake to the guest list."

He turned back to Griffin. "See you at four."

* * *

Griffin paced in the hot Los Angeles sun until he felt dizzy and dehydrated. The lack of information, Claus's smug face—it was crazy-making. He wanted to call someone, to get some reassurance, but no one came to mind. Daisy still wasn't returning his calls, and that made sense; Claus knew about the project, Claus *owned* the damn project, and he was toying with Griffin because he knew how much it meant to him.

Two million dollars. He didn't have two million dollars or anything close.

Fear gripped him.

He sent a text to Jim saying he'd had to run to LA for business but would be back later that night. He prayed that would be true.

* * *

At three forty-five, Griffin all but staggered back into Claus's office. His mind was awash with worry and a thousand and one possibilities of who might be in the office, but when he saw the clean-cut young man sitting on the sofa with an older gentleman, he nearly keeled over.

Tripp Ingersoll was sitting there, plain as day, dressed like a stockbroker without a care in the world.

Griffin did a double take.

Tripp just nodded politely and went back to his *Forbes* magazine. The man next to him, who smelled like a lawyer, tapped away on his BlackBerry with a stylus.

Dawn stood up and gestured toward the door. "You can all go in now."

Claus was still at his computer, but he quickly pushed it aside when Griffin, Tripp, and the lawyer entered the room.

"Gentlemen!" He gestured to the small round conference table near the window. "Come, sit down. Dawn, bring in the refreshments."

Griffin staggered into a chair and sat down hard. He couldn't stop staring at Tripp, the man who'd killed Carmen Kelly. Here, in this room.

In a meeting with Griffin. About the Kelly project.

Claus made introductions and small talk; after Dawn left, he stirred his coffee and stared pointedly at Griffin.

"Well, I'm glad this worked out for us to all speak about the Kelly project," Claus began.

"He's involved," Griffin said, blinking in surprise.

"I already have a book coming out—you know, telling my side of the story." Tripp opened a bottle of water. "The whole prosecution and the suffering my family went through because of that asshole cop."

Griffin's blood pressure jumped dangerously.

"But Claus called me with this cool idea. Like sort of an O.J. thing." He took a drag of water. "Like, I'm not saying I did it, but what if…you know?"

"What if?" Griffin leaned forward. "The screenplay doesn't include the actual murder."

"I think it should." Claus tapped on the table with his knuckles. "More dramatic. Otherwise it's just a dull trial film."

"It's about the family."

"Boring," Claus said, and Tripp laughed. Actually laughed. Griffin wanted to punch him in the face.

"We'll also be optioning Tripp's book for a movie, so in all honesty—once the screenplays are finished, I'll make a final decision about which one we'll actually make…"

The floor dropped out from under Griffin.

"Or just combine them," Claus finished.

Tripp was nodding. The lawyer was nodding.

Griffin stood up. "I need to leave."

"Griffin, don't be so dramatic. You can write the Kelly script. I'll get someone else to do Tripp's side of the story. Then we'll see what we have in a few months."

"I'd really like you to reconsider selling me the rights." Griffin stayed as calm as he possibly could.

"Come to me with two million dollars, and we'll talk."

* * *

Griffin stormed out of the office and headed for the gate. Andy, a security guard he knew fairly well, called him a cab. He didn't want to use a Bright Side car. He didn't want any more blood on his hands.

He gave the driver Daisy's address in Bel Air, dialing Jules's cell as they headed onto the freeway.

"Jules, it's Griff."

"Griffin! Where the blazes have you been? Daisy's been a fucking nightmare the past week!"

"I don't care. Where is she?"

"At the house far as I know. She's been hiding in her room for days."

"Thanks." Griffin hung up without another word. He leaned back into the pleather seat and tried to regain his breath.

* * *

Freida, the housekeeper, let him in. Her face was set in a disapproving line, clearly as annoyed with him as Jules was for not being around to "handle" Daisy. He ignored her and headed upstairs for the master bedroom.

Daisy's bedroom, as Claus had slept in the guest room for years.

"Daisy, open the goddamn door," he yelled. "I will kick it down, so help me God."

A second later the lock rattled and the double doors opened to reveal Daisy in her nightgown, her long red hair tangled around her shoulders.

She looked like shit.

"What?" she asked, and he could see the bright red eyes and drawn skin. She'd been crying for days, most likely, and self-medicating.

"What do you mean what? Do you know who I just had a meeting with, Daisy? Claus and Tripp fucking Ingersoll. Not only is this project now Claus's, he's putting in the point of view of the fucking murderer." Griffin squeezed every word out through a tight chest. "Do you know what you've done?"

"I'm sorry," Daisy murmured. She turned her back on him and walked slowly back to the bed.

"Sorry? No—that doesn't cut it. You have to help me."

"Help you what? I can't do anything—Claus owns everything…"

"He says he'll give me the project for two million. If I sell my car and my condo and the place in Aspen, I can raise some of that. Do you have any money we can use up front? Anything at all that's just yours?"

"No." Daisy crawled into the giant bed, under the silky peach comforter. "I don't have anything."

"Daisy, please. Please stay with me here. I need your help. I have no one else to go to," he pleaded. He climbed onto the bed, pulling at the covers to get her attention.

"I'm sorry," she repeated. He could hear the slight slur to her words.

"Daisy, Daisy—come on. Think."

"Fine." She forced herself upright, swaying against his shoulder. "Give me the phone."

Hands shaking, Griffin handed her the cordless from the nightstand. She dialed a number slowly, then raised the phone to her ear.

"Jules? It's Daisy. No, I'm fine. Yes, he's here. Listen, I need you to pull out those legal papers from the safe. The ones in the blue envelope. Right. Bring them over here as soon as possible. Okay. Yeah, I'm fine. Don't worry."

She hung up and turned to Griffin, her face haggard. "I'll get you the money, okay?"

"Promise?"

"Don't you trust me, Griffin?"

"Please don't make me answer that right now." Griffin slid off the bed, adrenaline letdown beating through his chest.

"I am sorry I lied to you, Griffin, I really am. You're my only friend in the world."

Griffin shook his head. "I don't think you know how to be a friend, Daisy. If this is how you treat me…"

"I was scared, okay? He was going to leave me for that woman!"

"And that isn't what you wanted? Fuck your career, Daisy—don't you want to be happy?" He threw his hands up.

"My career is all I have."

Griffin shook his head. "Okay, fine. Have your career and your shitty marriage."

"I have you, Griffin. That makes it all so much easier…"

Griffin looked at her sadly. "You don't have me anymore."

* * *

He couldn't stay.

She cried and cried but swore she'd make everything all right with Claus and with the project. He wanted to believe her, to believe that something of their long history together meant something of value.

Griffin called another taxi and went back to his house, head in his hands.

Chapter Twenty-one

"Jim? Could I see you in my office?"

Their new captain, Ellen Trainer, stuck her head in the break room where Jim and Terry were eating. They exchanged glances; then Jim followed her, wiping his face with a napkin as he went.

"Everything okay, Captain?" he asked. She gestured a chair, and that's when he noticed the PD lawyer sitting on her couch. "Okay, guessing not okay."

"Jim, this is Frank Seifer. We just wanted to let you know that a lawsuit has been filed by Tripp Ingersoll and his family against the department. You're named in the suit."

A loud buzzing noise filled Jim's head. He blinked a few times and nodded, both shocked and totally unsurprised.

"Took long enough," he said mildly.

Captain Trainer looked over at the lawyer. "You'll be covered by the PBA, of course. I just wanted to give you a heads-up."

"You'll settle before it goes to trial, I'm sure," Jim said, giving a glance over at the lawyer as well. "I can't imagine the department or the city wanting that much publicity."

"His lawyers have already mentioned they don't want a settlement," Seifer said. "I think while we would like to avoid publicity, Mr. Ingersoll would like as much as possible."

Jim snapped his fingers. "Ahhh, book deal, I'm guessing. Also wondered why that didn't happen sooner."

He sighed deeply. How much did he not want to deal with this?

"Are you going to be all right?" Captain Trainer was a nice person and clearly concerned with his well-being. Suddenly Jim felt just as concerned.

He couldn't do this. He didn't want to do this.

"Actually, I'm going to talk to my union rep about retirement options." The words left his lips, and he felt his face erupt in as much surprise as Captain Trainer's.

"That's your option, of course. It won't prevent you from testifying, however," Seifer offered.

"I know. But I won't be here, not on duty. Maybe it'll take some of the heat off." Jim shrugged. He really didn't care, so long as he didn't have to deal with it.

"I'm a little surprised, Jim. I thought you'd be furious and aiming for a fight."

Jim shrugged. "Life's too short."

* * *

Jim got back to his desk and sat down. He stared at his phone and his blotter and his neatly organized files. He'd

been sitting here for over ten years, with the departm
twenty. He was a very good cop.

Could he walk away? Just get up and retire and live a li
of leisure? Did he know what leisure was?

Maybe Griffin could teach him.

Maybe he'd go to LA and work on his tan.

Okay, probably not.

"You all right, man?" Terry hurried over to his desk, looking over his shoulder. "What's going on?"

"Lawsuit. Ingersoll's family." Jim rubbed his eyes. "I'm named."

"Am I…" Terry shook his head. "Sorry."

"No, no, I totally understand—you're not named, so far as I can tell. I'm pretty sure he only wants to ruin me."

"Shit, that's just so ridiculous." Terry fumed. "Anything I can do?"

"No, not right now." Jim thought for a long moment. "How'd you feel about getting another partner?"

"Shut up, you jerk. I'm not abandoning you…"

"Maybe I'm abandoning you."

Terry's eyes widened. "What?"

"I'm thinking about retirement, Terry. I'm thinking about it long and hard."

Terry sat down in Jim's visitor chair. "Seriously?"

"Very seriously."

"You're still young. You got plenty of years left to travel or…whatever. You'd have to get a hobby, though."

ld go to Hollywood and consult. I don't

exactly."

193

of time sitting around a pool. So after
give me a call and find me a job like

Jim smiled. "You're a good cop; you need to stay right here."

Terry ducked his head. "Thanks. But, uh—to be honest, I'm thinking about stuff too."

"Leaving?"

"Transferring. It's just, with the new baby, I don't want to be gone all the time. I don't like going home now with all this ugly stuff in my head—I can't imagine when my kid is there, waiting for me, and all I can think of is dead bodies and cruelty and…you know."

"Do what you need to, okay? You want me to make some calls, give you references, whatever. No problems." Jim felt relieved at the possibility of not leaving Terry totally behind.

"Wow."

"Yeah, wow."

His phone rang, and Jim grabbed it up. "Jim Shea."

"Jim? It's Pete Van Dell."

Ed Kelly's closest neighbor.

"Hey, Pete, what's going on?"

"I just wanted to let you know that I had to drive Ed to the hospital this mornin'. He wasn't feeling well, so I insisted. I wanted to give you a call…"

Jim's stomach clenched. "I'll be up there as soon as I can."

* * *

Jim texted Griffin as he sped up the highway to Tacoma. *Ed sick. Home????*
He didn't get a response.

* * *

The doctor came out of Ed's room and spotted Jim sitting in one of the plastic chairs in the hallway.

"Detective Shea?"

"Yes?"

"Doctor Pah." The man shook Jim's hand. His face had a kindly aura, and Jim knew there was bad news coming. "I won't waste any time telling you the outcome…"

"How long?"

"A few days, possibly a week." Dr. Pah pressed the chart under his arm. "He's comfortable. We'll do whatever we can to manage his pain, monitor him."

Jim nodded. He'd been waiting for this for months, and now it seemed a complete and total shock. Reality hitting his face at about fifty miles an hour.

"Thank you. May I go in?"

"Absolutely. I'll leave a note at the front desk that you are next of kin and should be allowed in whenever you'd like."

Jim shook the man's hand again and slipped into the room. Ed was awake, his head turned to look out of the window to his left.

"Hey, Ed."

"Jim! They get you out of work for this?" Ed clucked his tongue. "Told 'em to wait till you got off."

"It's okay." Jim took a seat at his bedside. "You need anything?"

Ed squinted toward the window again. "Nah. The company's nice, though, gotta admit."

"I'll stay as long as you need me to."

"Saying it again, Jim, even though I know you don't like it. You're a good man."

"Stop."

"Griffin gonna come up and visit?"

"I don't think you're up to working right now, Ed."

"Workin'? Nah, I just want to see him again. He's a nice young man, Jim—you picked a good one."

Jim rubbed his forehead. "We're just dating…"

"Uh-huh." Ed smirked. "That's what I told my friends about Della. They laughed at me."

"They sound rude," Jim said drily. "But apparently I have the same friends."

"Good for you, then. Friends and those you love, that's the most important stuff in life. You gotta get 'em and keep 'em and never stop saying how much you love 'em. Life's too short."

Ed sighed. "'Course, I'm lucky…"

"Lucky?" Jim blurted out. "Sorry."

"Don't be sorry. I know people don't understand how I can say that. But man, I'll tell you—I know so many people who never loved anyone like I loved Della. And they never appreciated their kids like I appreciated my Carmen. I feel sad for them, Jim, I do. For all the ugliness, I'd do it one more time just to be with my girls again."

* * *

Ed slept. Jim watched. He rolled Ed's words over and over in his head, trying to understand. Even with everything he'd gone through, he refused to be bitter or closed off.

Refused.

Jim hid himself in a box and hadn't had one hundredth of the trials Ed had.

Refused to live.

His phone buzzed. Jim saw a text message and read it.

What do you need? Griffin's text asked.

Jim's hand wavered slightly.

You, was his answer.

Soon. I promise.

Jim put his phone away and went back to watching Ed sleep.

Chapter Twenty-two

Ed's daytime nurse was named Frances. She and Ed chatted when he was conscious and she had time, and Jim appreciated the updates she gave whenever he showed up or called during the three days Ed had been in the hospital.

When he walked up to the nurses' station early Saturday morning and Frances had tears in her eyes, he didn't need a report in words or specifics.

"Not much more time," she murmured, taking his arm and ushering him toward the door to Ed's room. "He didn't want me to call anyone…" Her voice trailed off, as she clearly waited for Jim to fill in the blanks, but he shook his head.

"There's no one but me," Jim muttered and went into the room alone.

Ed was lying motionless under the pale blue blanket, even more skeletal than yesterday and hooked to oxygen and an IV.

Jim paused as the door swished closed at his back. For a terrible moment he wished it were already over, so he didn't have to say good-bye, but Ed's chest moved up and down as if to remind him there was still time.

He walked over and sat down quietly to wait for some sign that Ed knew he was here. When too many ticks of the clock passed, Jim laid his hand on the blanket near Ed's arm.

Time ticked away as Jim counted the seconds between inhalations and exhalations under the blanket. He lost track of everything but the counting until he blinked and realized the shadows in the room had deepened across them both.

The door opened a second later, and Jim almost jerked away from Ed but forced himself to stay still. He thought it was Frances or the doctor, but a whiff of aftershave turned his head in complete surprise.

Griffin stood in the doorway, hands in the pockets of his khakis and a sad look on his face.

Hi, he mouthed, indicating Ed with a tilt of his head.

"Sleeping," Jim murmured, a feeling of relief and pain intermingling in his chest. He couldn't imagine anyone he wanted to see more in the world at this moment, and it was terrifying.

Griffin walked over, grabbing the second chair in the room and bringing it next to Jim's. He butted the two chairs together, so when he sat down, his thigh matched up against Jim's.

"You need anything?" he whispered as he looked over at Ed's sleeping form.

Jim stared at Griffin's profile, then cleared his throat, realizing he had to answer. "Nothing," he answered, and it was the gospel truth.

"You need to eat or drink at least." Griffin sat back in the seat and reached into the pocket of his blazer to pull out a small bottle of water. "I'll get you coffee and some dinner in a few minutes."

"I ate..."

"Breakfast. Maybe lunch?" Griffin gave him a small smile. "Shut up and let me do something nice for you."

Jim didn't have any words at that moment; he simply blinked and went back to counting Ed's breaths.

Griffin sat beside him for a few hundred more clicks of the clock, then murmured something about coffee. He disappeared briefly, eventually returning with the aforementioned hot beverage in the largest cup Jim had seen in a while.

"There's a sandwich when you're ready," Griffin said, handing the cup over as he sat back down.

"Yes, dear," Jim mumbled, but he smiled as he took a sip.

Francis came and went over the next few hours, tidying the room and indulging the boys with smiles. The last time around, her smile didn't last long as she took Ed's pulse; it didn't take a medical degree to read her expression.

She said she'd get the doctor, and Griffin didn't push the sandwich anymore.

"Do you want me to leave?" Griffin asked as soon as she left.

"No, why would I?"

Griffin didn't respond, but Jim could see he was pleased.

Which in turn helped Jim breathe a little bit easier for the moment.

"You should, uh—I don't know. If you're gonna say something, you should say it soon." Griffin's face twisted up for a second as he stared down at the floor.

Jim put the coffee cup on the bedside table. He knew Griffin was talking urgency—because Ed didn't have long, and he remembered the story Griffin told him about his mother.

He stood up and leaned over Ed's still form; he moved without thinking, which is the only way he could get out of that chair.

A flurry of words started to whirl in Jim's head. Apologies for Carmen's case, words for all Ed had taught him and given him in the time they'd known one another. Words he knew he could never say aloud about the father Ed was, whether he knew it or not—Carmen was his failure in some ways, but Jim…Jim might be counted as his success.

"Ed," he murmured, his voice halting and strained. A gentle touch against the back of his leg steadied him a bit. "Ed, thank you. Thank you so much."

The door opened and Jim looked up to see the doctor, who seemed apologetic for interrupting.

"Come in," he said as he breathed in deeply and walked away from the bedside to give the doctor some room to work. And over to the window to give himself a break.

Jim stared out into the parking lot of the hospital. He tracked a few cars coming and going, some dark clouds moving in over the mountains that promised rain. He didn't turn his head when Griffin came to stand next to him, but he didn't resist the gentle touch of his lover's hand in his.

The doctor cleared his throat to get their attention.

Jim turned around and read the doctor's expression as well as he'd read Francis's.

"If we could stay…"

The doctor nodded. "Of course. Just call the nurses' station if you need anything."

That was all that needed to be said. That could be said. Everyone shared another round of pained faces, and the doctor left.

It was just waiting game now.

* * *

Griffin fell asleep in one of the leatherette chairs near the window about an hour later. Jim ate his cold ham-and-cheese sandwich, finished his equally cold coffee. Ed didn't wake; Griffin didn't stir. Jim felt some comfort in the routine of gentle snores and clock ticking, even as he strained to hear Ed's labored breathing.

It was taking longer for the blanket to rise and fall.

Jim checked the clock and saw it was almost one o'clock. He thought about waking Griffin and sending him back to Ed's house to sleep more comfortably, but selfishly, he wanted the other man here. Close enough to see and touch and need when the time came.

The time was coming.

In a perfect world, in a movie, Ed would have woken up and said something profound. Given Jim his blessing and love and gone out with wise words on his lips. But at half past one he took a deep, painful breath, so sharp that the sound made Griffin stir on the other side of the room.

Jim got up and leaned over Ed, gripping his hand tightly. He remembered Carmen's body in that empty parking lot and Della's body in the back of that ambulance and squeezed until sweat dotted his forehead.

He wanted Ed to know he was here. He wanted Ed to remember he wasn't alone at this moment.

He held on for a few more heartbeats—his own racing heart pounding in his ears as Ed's slowed and slowed. He swore he could feel the last pulse before a machine signaled that it was over.

Jim couldn't let go.

Even though everything had changed, he couldn't relax his hand or stand up straight. The door opened, and he heard quiet voices, and he still didn't move.

"You did great," a voice whispered in his ear. "You helped him go. Now just let these guys take over, okay?"

Griffin's arms were around him, urging him to move away from Ed's body. He didn't pull or tug or force the issue, but the embrace and the gentle pressure made it easier for Jim to let go, to relax the muscles of his hands and straighten his back. And eventually, to step away.

* * *

There were a few papers to sign, things to discuss. So much had already been decided that it was just a matter of going over the details.

Griffin stood silently at Jim's side through it all. At some point he managed to disappear, buy a large bottle of cold water, and reappear again before Jim noticed at all. Two hours after Ed had finally passed, Jim found himself in the passenger side of his truck as Griffin drove slowly out of the hospital parking lot.

"Uh—sorry, but…Ed's house? A hotel? Which would you prefer?" he asked softly.

Jim rubbed his face hard with both hands, trying to kick himself out of the funk and find an answer. Everything seemed fuzzy and out of focus; he heard Griffin, he knew what was going on, but thinking seemed out of the realm of possibility.

When he didn't answer, Griffin seemed to make a decision on his own. He pulled out onto the dark highway and turned up the heat before resting a hand on Jim's knee.

Comforting without saying anything. When they pulled into Ed's driveway, it seemed exactly the right answer.

* * *

Griffin made coffee and brought it into the spare room where Jim was already in bed. Jim walked through the door, into the room, and stripped down without speaking or thinking much. Crawling into the freshly made bed felt comforting and sad at once.

Jim lay on his side, facing the wall. The small television was on a local news channel, the sound low. He didn't turn over when Griffin came in, but he did roll a bit closer when his boyfriend got into bed.

"Need anything?" Griffin asked.

Jim could smell the coffee, feel the warm length of Griffin's body next to him.

"No, thanks," he said softly.

Griffin didn't say anything, but his hand, warm from the coffee cup, rested against Jim's hip. Holding him steady until he fell asleep.

Chapter Twenty-three

"Terry Oh."

"Hey, Terry—this is Griffin Drake…"

"Hi, hi." Terry paused. "Crap. Bad news, I'm guessing."

"Yeah." Griffin sighed deeply. "Last night. Jim's still asleep. I was just going to make the calls before he wakes up so he doesn't have to deal with it."

"That's pretty nice of you, Griffin."

"It's the least I could do."

"Let me know about the funeral arrangements. I'm not sure Mimi can travel, but I'll be there. You want me to talk to Nick and Heather?"

"Thanks—that would be helpful. I'm going to call Ben next, because there's going to be more legal stuff, I'm sure." Griffin tapped his BlackBerry stylus on the scarred kitchen table, making the little spilled drops of Splenda dance on the surface. "Not sure if there's anyone else."

"If I think of anyone, I'll let you know. Tell Jim I have things under control here and not to rush back."

"You've met Jim, right?"

Terry laughed. "Point taken. Thanks for calling."

"No problem."

Griffin hung up and picked up his coffee. It was cup number five since the pot last night as he attempted to watch over Jim and get some stuff done without falling into a deep coma himself. He monitored his e-mail and messages religiously, worried that Claus would break his promise when news of Ed Kelly's death reached his ears.

Daisy had talked to Claus that night as Griffin fretted in his apartment; he paced and packed and sent e-mails to real estate agents in LA and Aspen, put an ad for his car on the local Craigslist. She called him in the morning as he agonized over Ed's turn for the worse and his inability to be there with Jim.

She swore it was a done deal. She made a deal with Claus for the rights to the film. He'd be getting paperwork shortly.

He thanked her again and again, but she hung up without another word.

Then he waited for the official notification from Bright Side, which hadn't yet come when he flew out of LA to get back to Tacoma and Jim.

So far nothing seemed to have changed. Claus promised him the project. Daisy swore it. She would presumably front the money until he could come up with it. The fat lady was warming up to sing her final few notes as soon as the legal paperwork finally arrived with signatures in place.

Exhaustion crept up and knocked on the door, pushing him into a foggy delirium as he checked his messages one more time. Maybe if he laid his head down for ten minutes—max—he could make it a few more hours…

* * *

Griffin woke up with a start.

He smelled bacon and eggs.

There was a blanket on his shoulders; as he sat up it slid off, and his entire back cracked so loudly, there was an actual echo.

"Heavens! I knew sleeping in that chair wasn't a good idea," a voice said, and Griffin looked over to see an older woman in an apron standing over the stove with a spatula in her hand. "Are you all right, young man?"

"Uh...yes, ma'am." Griffin stretched and twisted until he could move without breaking the sound barrier. "Sorry about that."

"Oh no, don't apologize. You were so tired," she said sympathetically. "I'm Carla Kelly."

"Griffin Drake. I'm sorry—are you a relative of Ed's?"

"Second cousin by marriage. We got a call from Jim this morning and got right in the car." She shook her head. "So sad, but at least they're all together now, Ed and Della and Carmen." She turned back to the stove, and Griffin shook his head to clear the cobwebs. Jim? Morning? He looked over at the rooster-shaped clock and saw it was three thirty in the afternoon.

"Is Jim around?"

"He had some errands to run, he said. I think he'll be back soon. Guessing you're hungry—eggs and bacon all right?"

"Yeah, thanks. That would be great, actually." Griffin flipped open his computer to check his e-mail, then grabbed his BlackBerry. Nothing.

OhGodohGodohGod.

He flashed back to the meeting in Claus's office, face-to-face with Tripp Ingersoll, and felt the cold sweat breaking under his hair.

"Here you go," Carla said cheerfully. She put the plate in front of Griffin along with a mug of coffee. It was the world's best dad mug that Ed had been holding the first time they were here, where Griffin swore that they would do nothing to harm the memories of Carmen or Della.

Oh God.

He didn't know what to do besides choke down the breakfast Ed's second cousin by marriage dropped in front of him. He drank the coffee and cleaned his plate and then politely excused himself to shower and change.

And freak and pray with hands shaking as he disappeared into the bathroom to dial Daisy's cell phone.

Griffin sat on the toilet seat, the door closed behind him. Everything in the tiny guest bathroom smelled lavender, the wallpaper covered with tiny purple pictures of it. He thought this might have been Carmen's bathroom, and how much did he now wish they'd gone to a damn hotel.

"Hello?" she said coolly through the phone, startling him into attention.

"Daisy? Thank God. I—Claus hasn't sent the papers yet."

There was a long pause. "He said he would. It's out of my hands now."

"What? Jesus, Daisy—Ed Kelly died last night, okay? He's dead. I need to know that the papers are signed and legal and everything is taken care of. I made a promise, and I intend to keep it."

"He's dead?" Her voice was small. "Oh, Griffin, I'm sorry. How's Jim?"

"Devastated. A state that will not be helped if he finds out what Claus wanted to do with this movie." Griffin raked a hand through his hair, pulling hard.

"He doesn't know?"

"No, he doesn't. I didn't feel it would go over too well mentioning me in the same room with Tripp Fucking Ingersoll."

"Griffin, calm down. I'll find out if Claus sent the papers and call you back, okay?"

"Please, Daisy. Please," was all he could manage before hanging up, the shakes moving to small earthquakes.

He sat there for a few minutes more and thought about all the ways this could get ugly. All the ways he could disappoint Jim and make everything he'd said about this project a giant lie.

People were talking outside the door; he heard Jim's voice and stood up quickly, turned on the shower to give himself some time. He stripped down and got into the cold sputtering spray, praying like he hadn't prayed since childhood that Daisy would call back soon.

She didn't call.

He dried off and wrapped a towel around his waist; phone in hand, he darted out of the bathroom and into the guest room for some clean clothes.

Jim walked in as he was buttoning up his jeans.

"Hey," he said wearily. Jim was shaved and dressed in a suit, his face pinched and exhausted.

"Hi. How are you doing?" Griffin's heart was banging in his chest, but he couldn't stop himself from going over and wrapping his arms around Jim, pulling him into a tight embrace.

"Shitty but okay. You get some sleep?"

"Conked out on the kitchen table. Carla made me breakfast."

"She's a nice lady." Jim hugged him back, tight and strong, and Griffin didn't want to let go. "She and ladies from her church are making food for the wake. Ed didn't want anything with an open casket or a graveside burial, but we're doing a little thing here."

"I called Terry. He was going to let everyone else know."

"Thanks." Jim pressed a kiss to Griffin's cheek. He pulled away before Griffin was ready to let him go. "I'll see you out there—I have mingling to do." He looked distinctly displeased at the prospect, but for Ed, Griffin knew he'd do anything.

He disappeared out the door again, and Griffin checked his BlackBerry.

Nothing.

* * *

Neighbors and acquaintances grouped in Ed's living room, coffee cups in hand as they talked in hushed tones and sampled a spread of cakes on the kitchen table.

Jim brought Griffin around and introduced him; he didn't say "boyfriend" or anything, but the way he held on to his arms raised enough eyebrows—literally—for Griffin to know the point was made. Apparently "Ed's gay friends" were a well-gossiped point. No one was rude, however, and they shook his hand, expressed their condolences. Numb by now, Griffin wandered around, ate some cake, drank too much coffee, and touched his pocket every ten seconds to see if it was vibrating.

The afternoon wound on. The ladies, under Carla's supervision, served a luncheon. Griffin excused himself to hyperventilate in the bedroom, then called Daisy's cell. Voice mail. Same with the phone in her office. He tried Jules and got all her voice mails as well.

This didn't bode well.

Balls in hand, he called Claus next, but his assistant refused to put him through, insisting that Claus couldn't be disturbed. She sounded far more stressed than usual.

Griffin hung up and rejoined the mourners.

* * *

It was eight before the last guest trickled out and Carla cleaned the kitchen. She promised to be back tomorrow morning to cook them breakfast and get things ready for the wake; Jim walked her to her car like a true gentleman, leaving Griffin to watch from the screen door.

"She's like…a professional," Jim said as he walked up the stairs. Griffin opened the door for him.

"Church ladies are professionals, Jim. This is what they train for. Illness and birth and death and potluck suppers." Griffin's voice was affectionate. Carla reminded him of home and his dad.

"Well, thank God she's around, because there were a lot of people here." He pulled at his tie and jacket and headed for the living room. "I haven't talked that much in years."

"You're actually pretty good at chitchat." Griffin followed Jim like his shadow, practically ending up in his lap on the sofa.

"Eh. I guess I picked it up from Ed."

"He was a great guy."

"The best."

"You're a great guy too."

"You all right?" Jim turned his head to look at Griffin. "I mean, I know this is a shitty day and all, but you seem jumpy."

"I don't like funerals and stuff," Griffin bluffed, laying his head on Jim's shoulder to avoid his gaze. "Plus I'm worried about you."

"I'll be okay. Promise. I think I prepared myself for it…"

"Listen, I have to tell you something." The words erupted from Griffin's mouth before he could stop them.

"What?" Concern settled into the worried creases on Jim's face. He looked like he'd aged ten years in forty-eight hours. He was exhausted. He was sad. He'd just spent hours entertaining a house full of people who knew Ed, to honor his memory.

Griffin loved him so much it hurt.

"I know this is like the worst possible time, but I really need to tell you that I love you. Okay? Because I do. And you don't have to say it back or anything, but that's how it is."

"Oh." Jim looked gobsmacked, and Griffin threw himself backward on the couch with a moan.

"Sorry."

"What are you apologizing for? I'm just surprised, that's it." Jim tugged at Griffin in an attempt to get him to sit up. "C'mere."

"No." Griffin's hand went to his pocket again, but nothing. No vibration. "Fine."

He sat up and let Jim manhandle him into an awkward embrace.

"So…no one's really ever said that to me, so, you know…I'm surprised." Jim cleared his throat. "And, ah—not really ever said it back."

"You don't have to."

"I know. But you gotta know—it's there."

Griffin's eyes widened. "Seriously?"

"Seriously." Jim actually blushed. Griffin fell another ten leagues in love.

"Wow. Shit."

"Romantic dialogue really hits the spot."

"Dialogue? What, are you dating a screenwriter or something?"

"Apparently." Jim kissed him, then, and Griffin forgot to check his phone for the rest of the night.

Chapter Twenty-four

Mimi didn't make it—doctor's orders—but Terry, Heather, and Nick drove up from Seattle. Ben and Liddy were in court, but they sent a basket of flowers and a card along with the Power Cabal representatives.

"Happy Monday?" Jim said as Terry walked up and shook his hand.

"Suckass Monday." Terry gave him a one-armed hug. "How you holding up, partner?"

"Eh." Heather came up and gave Jim a big hug, then a second.

"One was from Mimi. She's mad she couldn't come."

"She's incubating—she shouldn't be getting upset or sitting in a car that long."

"Incubating?"

"Sorry, I hung out with a lot of farmers yesterday."

They went into the house and found Carla in the kitchen feeding Griffin a second plate of pancakes. He mouthed, *Save me*, then got up to say hello to everyone.

Jim liked the way his friends and Griffin chatted over breakfast. He watched them over his coffee cup, thought about Griffin's words last night.

He had known it was coming because he felt it himself. He thought he would be more freaked out, but maybe the dull ache of loss evened out all emotions.

He would miss Ed, very much. But if there was one lesson he'd learned from the man, it was dwelling on the negative wasted time. Wasted your life. Jim was forty-five years old and done with wasting precious time. He could go back to work and catch the wrong end of a bullet or stroke out in the gym. He could fall or get sick or a million other things, and there would be nothing to show for his life except a nice personnel folder and some money stuck in a bank.

And a pending lawsuit from an asshole.

What the hell kind of life was that?

"Jim? Yo, Jim," Nick said, snapping his fingers in front of Jim's face. "Your phone is ringing."

"What? Sorry." He pulled his phone out of his pocket and said, "Jim Shea."

"Jim? Hi, it's Liddy."

"Hi, Liddy. Hey, thanks for the flowers. That was real nice."

"No problem. Listen, I'm on recess at the moment, but my secretary called to say there were legal papers dropped off at our office regarding the movie from Bright Side Studios..."

"Really? I wonder what for?" Jim looked over at Griffin and signaled for his attention.

"Not sure. I wasn't expecting anything, but they look like changes to the original contract. I'm going to have her read them over, then call me back. Just wanted to give you a heads-up."

"Thanks, Liddy." Griffin excused himself and joined Jim on the far side of the table. "Call me when you know something."

"What's up?" Griffin asked as Jim hung up.

"Liddy said the studio sent over some papers about the movie—changes to the contract? Any idea what they're about?"

Griffin's face went pure white, and Jim got to his feet in a split second, worried his boyfriend was going to hit the floor.

"Uh, no...no, let me make some calls and I'll see," he said hurriedly, then jetted out of the room like he was on fire.

"Be right back," Jim said absently, following Griffin outside to the driveway, where he found the other man frantically dialing a number on his phone.

"What's wrong?"

"Nothing; go back inside. I'll take care of it." Griffin paced farther down the driveway. "Daisy? Pick up now; I mean it."

There was a pause; then Griffin cursed, redialing. "Seriously, Jim, it's nothing. Go inside."

"It's clearly not nothing..." Jim took a few steps toward Griffin.

"Dawn? Put Claus on the phone right now. I mean it. Right this second. I don't care about meetings... Where is he? Home—are you sure?" He hung up again and dialed, not even looking up at Jim this time.

"Freida? It's Griffin. I need to talk to Claus or Daisy right this second." He paused and walked farther away from Jim. "This can't wait; it's an emergency."

"Claus? There was a deal in place. Daisy told me there was a deal in place—I will get you your money, but we had a deal! Does that mean nothing to you?" Griffin kept going down the driveway and Jim followed; his stomach dropped to his knees. "I gave you every concession…"

He paced in a circle.

"You know what? Fuck you. Fuck you. I want my contract canceled. I want nothing from you—no money, nothing. Zero. Just give me my project and leave me alone."

Jim stopped dead in his tracks.

"You can't do this, Claus. You can't do this to the Kellys…"

Griffin's face turned red.

"'They're all dead so it doesn't matter'? That's your answer? Apparently that was the last answer, because Griffin hurled his BlackBerry across the yard. It bounced off a tree and went into a dozen pieces.

He sat down hard in the middle of the driveway, head in his hands.

Jim's feet unfroze as he walked to Griffin, the one-sided conversation replaying over and over in his head.

"What's going on?" he murmured as he knelt down next to Griffin on the driveway.

"I fucked up. I swear I didn't know." Griffin moaned, pulling at his hair. "Daisy signed everything over to him. He wants to make a movie... He wants Tripp's point of view... Oh God, I sat in an office with that murderer, and Claus wants me to work with him..."

"What?" Jim pushed down the urge to grab Griffin and shake him.

"I know, I know. I tried to buy it back. I offered him everything I had, and he told Daisy yes, but now..." Griffin was almost crying now, but Jim couldn't get over his own red-eyed anger over his boyfriend in a room with Tripp Ingersoll—without telling him.

"We'll sue him."

"We can't."

"Then I'll break his legs."

Griffin laughed/cried into his knees. "Break mine first. This is my fault."

"Jim?" Heather was calling him from the house. "There's a call for Griffin on the landline..."

"Come on," Jim said, his hand under Griffin's armpit as he lifted him up.

"It's someone named Daisy Mae," Heather said helpfully.

* * *

Griffin took Daisy's call in the bedroom while Jim paced the living room. Mourners and friends were arriving, so he distracted himself with another round of small talk, helping

Carla and her church ladies carry the boxes of food and drink into the kitchen.

He tried not to obsess over all this, but it wasn't easy. He wanted to scream and kick down the bedroom door, find out what the hell was going on. The idea of this movie being made into a spectacle, the idea of Ed's family being raked over the coals like that. He stared at the room of dark-suited people and felt his heart break.

* * *

The minister from Ed's church arrived; Ed wasn't much of a churchgoer, Jim knew, but this man had married Ed and Della and baptized Carmen. He had said some words at their burials as well. He shook Jim's hand heartily.

"Ed spoke of you so often," Reverend Peller said. "He was as fond of you as if you were his own son."

Jim's throat closed up, and he nodded. "Thank you. That's quite an honor."

"You've done so much good for Ed, Jim. I don't think he'd mind me saying thank you and God bless."

Jim clapped the man on his arm and led him to rest of the crowd, unable to go further than a murmured "thank you." Terry caught him near the kitchen and pulled him to the back door.

"Listen, don't freak…"

"Oh, God almighty, what?"

"There are reporters outside. The truck just pulled up…"

"Terry, I swear I will rip their heads right off."

"I called the local sheriff, and he's coming out to deal with it. One of them was asking if I had a comment about the movie news, and I had no idea what he was talking about."

"There's some legal shit going on. Griffin's dealing with it," Jim lied/hoped.

"Okay. Just so you know."

"Right. Thanks, man." Jim left Terry to the reporters and headed for the back bedroom, determined to find out what was going on, on Griffin's end. The door was locked, so he knocked urgently.

"Griffin? There are reporters here," he mumbled through the crack.

The door unlocked, and Griffin stood there looking shocked, as if he'd seen Ed's ghost on the other side of the doorway. "What?"

"Reporters…here. We called the sheriff."

"Hang on," he said into the receiver. "There are reporters here. Do you want to… Yeah? It's up to you. All right, Daisy Mae."

Griffin hung up.

"Daisy said she's taken care of everything this time. No screwups, no more games," Griffin said wearily. "I can't promise what that means, but she swore it."

"Do you trust her?"

"No. Maybe." Griffin shrugged. "I used to. Maybe I should one last time."

Jim tried to stay mad at Griffin, but nothing held fast; he pulled him into his arms as the other man shook with worry.

* * *

Nick and Terry went out when the sheriff arrived. The reporters didn't seem overly interested in what he was saying, all of them on their cell phones listening eagerly to news.

Jim stood near the door.

"Hey, is Griffin Drake in there?" one of the reporters called out. "He available for a statement about the announcement from Bright Side Studios?"

"Griffin!" Jim called into the house, his boyfriend appearing with a large tumbler of scotch in hand. "Someone said something about an announcement from the studio."

"How do I look?" Griffin asked, shoving his drink into Jim's hand and fixing his hair. He looked slightly disheveled but went out the door without waiting for an answer. Jim followed, stashing the scotch on the front steps.

"Griffin Drake here—someone looking for me?" Griffin called breezily.

"Hey, Steve Winzer, Entertainment Spotlight. I just got a call that said Bright Side is announcing they're moving operations to Germany in the next year, with all U.S. projects on hold or being sold off."

"I can confirm the move," Griffin said coolly.

"Are you still with the studio?"

"No, no. Taking my personal projects elsewhere. I of course wish Claus and Daisy and everyone at Bright Side Studios the best in their future endeavors."

"Of course." Steve laughed. "The Ed Kelly project moving ahead? I heard they optioned Ingersoll's book for a movie as well."

"No idea about that either. Except that the Ed Kelly project is moving ahead with another studio without any input from Tripp Ingersoll."

"Which one?"

"Oh, come on, Steve, like I'm giving you anything else. Call my agent, and we'll set up something when I make the official announcement."

"I'll take it." Steve shook Griffin's hand. "Thanks."

"No problem. Now the sheriff is going to kick you out. No hard feelings."

"I'm used to it."

His cool demeanor slipping, Griffin turned and walked past Jim.

"How much of that was bullshit?" Jim murmured, catching up with him.

"Like ninety-eight percent. I gotta get back on the phone. Oh, and call Liddy—tell her to shred whatever documents Bright Side sent over to the office."

Chapter Twenty-five

A few hours later, the house cleared out for the last time. People were carrying mementos Ed had carefully marked for them, plus leftovers. Heather, Nick, Terry, and Jim sat in the living room when the place finally emptied out, nursing the end of the coffee and cake.

"Is Griffin okay?" Terry asked finally.

"Business crap," was all Jim would say, but he nodded. "I think he'll be fine."

An hour later he said good-bye to his friends and found Griffin asleep on the bed, the phone lying next to him.

Jim got out of his suit and lay down next to him, exhaustion pricking at his eyelids even as he desperately wanted to know what was going on. An irrational part of him wanted to shake Griffin awake, but the drawn expression was impossible to miss.

He must've dozed, because movement on the bed caught his attention as his eyes opened.

Griffin was packing his bag.

"Where are you going?" Jim croaked as he sat up.

"Back to LA," Griffin said quietly. "I have some loose ends to tie up."

"Like what?"

"Like finding a studio for my project. Finding a part-time job. Valet or dog shampooing." He laughed, raw and tired.

Jim got off the bed.

"What happened?"

"I used every cent in my bank account to buy Ed's project, plus they now own my car, my condo, and the place in Aspen. Claus squeezed everything out of me he possibly could. Then I terminated my contract at Bright Side." He was talking to himself now, methodically putting himself and his bag together.

"Stop, stop." Jim put his hands on Griffin's shoulders and turned him around. "Stop, okay? You don't have to worry about money."

"Yeah, I kinda do." Griffin wouldn't look him in the eye.

"Griffin, I have money. I can give you what you need— hell, I'll give you the money back for Ed's movie, okay? And the no-contract thing—you wanted out, yeah? So you're out. Now you can change your career."

"She gave up everything," Griffin interrupted. He shook his head. "She gave up everything. I have stuff to sell. She's got nothing."

"She? Daisy?"

"She offered him a divorce—no fault. No alimony. Not even the fifty percent she's entitled to of the studio. Just so he would agree to my offer. Jules said she packed her suitcase and left, and no one knows where she is."

"Oh God." Jim felt the reality of the situation settling over him. "Listen…the important thing is you're out of there and you can make your own decisions now. Except for you leaving right now—I'm totally overruling that."

"Are you going to arrest me?"

"No, I'm using boyfriend's prerogative."

"Boyfriend?"

"It's late and I'm delirious. I make no promises about what words I use in the light of day."

* * *

Jim got them both undressed and into bed.

"Okay, I lied. I'll probably say boyfriend in the morning too."

"That's cool." Griffin paused, a dark shadow against Jim's shoulder. "Also, I still love you."

"Thanks."

"I'm sorry."

"Don't be."

"You don't even know why I'm saying it."

"It doesn't matter. Whatever it is, just don't be sorry. Life's too short."

* * *

It wasn't easy packing up and leaving Ed's house the next day. They'd be back, of course, to empty the house and finalize the sale, but the reality of Ed never being there, in his warm and cozy living room, offering coffee and cookies and quiet conversation—that couldn't be overlooked anymore.

His ashes were being interred at the gravesite where Della and Carmen were. Griffin asked about visiting, but Jim put it off. He needed to get back to his life as soon as possible before he decided never to leave.

The ride back was quiet. Griffin still seemed shell-shocked from his complete change of circumstance.

"I'm unemployed," he kept saying, seemingly at each mile marker, until the morose tone gave way to something lighter. More optimistic. "I'm an unemployed screenwriter."

"Luckily your boyfriend is a trust-fund baby."

"Hey, wait—it's daylight! You said boyfriend!" Griffin actually laughed then, and Jim felt his job was, for the moment, done.

* * *

When they got back to Seattle, it was late and Jim felt done. Stuck with a fork and finished off, wanting nothing more than some food and bed. The fact that Griffin was schlepping into the building with luggage and enough leftovers to feed the city made it seem much nicer than it would have otherwise.

"Let me put this stuff in the fridge…" Griffin yawned, leaving his luggage.

"Nah, let me. I'm hungry."

"Again?"

"You want me to fix you a plate?"

"Yes."

Griffin pulled two bottles of water and two beers out of the fridge—and a handful of napkins off the counter—and headed upstairs. Jim watched him go, and a thought happened into his mind, sauntering in with a casual stroll.

He belongs here.

Jim set out two plates and started filling them up. His brain darted about from worry to pleasure to a plan to another worry to that sheer panic induced when Jim thought about a close relationship.

"Hey, don't go crazy," Griffin called from above; Jim looked up to see his boyfriend peeking through the rails. "But you know that apple crumb-topped thing... There's some room on the plate."

"You want it warmed up?

"Nah. Get your ass up here."

When Jim got to the top step, Griffin was lying spread-eagle on the bed in his underwear, watching the ceiling fan.

"Seriously, I love your bed."

"It's a great bed. You should, uh...you should sleep in it more often."

Griffin raised his head. "Well, I *am* unemployed, so..."

Jim put the plates on the dresser. "Yeah. And you have no place to live. You could just...stay here. If you want."

"James Shea, did you just ask me to move in?"

"Too soon?"

"No. I mean—for you? Yeah, I'm guessing this is soon, but...you know, since you asked..."

"Is that a yes?"

"Yes. Just because I'm unemployed and homeless and all." Griffin sat up, his expression lighter than Jim had seen in days.

"Right. This is about saving money."

"And you clearly need someone to keep this place from falling into disrepair."

Jim smirked as he handed Griffin his plate. "I found a dust bunny the other day…"

"Oh, dear God. Someone call public health." Griffin scooted over enough to give Jim room.

"We're eating in bed again."

"I know. It's okay. Live dangerously."

Jim dug into the leftovers with occasional sips of the beer Griffin brought up. This was nice. He could get used to this.

He was used to this.

After they finished, Griffin took the plates downstairs. He threatened to wash them, just to show what a potentially good roommate he was, and Jim yelled, "Boyfriend!" and Griffin came back up, laughing.

Jim was never going to get tired of that.

"Come to bed," he said, and Griffin clearly knew he didn't mean to sleep. It'd been a long few days of stolen kisses, and both of them needed more.

"Nothing crazy, I have a metric ton of food in my stomach," Griffin muttered, lying on top of Jim and nuzzling his jaw.

"Romantic."

"Reality." Griffin kissed him then, long and lewd, opening his mouth and twisting their tongues together with hot pressure. His hands drifted up to hold Jim's head in place, not letting him have any control over the kiss, forcing him to take it.

That was the sort of reality Jim wanted. His hips bucked up as he reached down to hold Griffin's hips in place. Two could play this game—and they could both benefit.

Jim rolled them to their sides, kicking away the blanket and sheet. Their legs found a perfect scissor after a second of fumbling, hard and urgent thrusts as Griffin fucked his mouth with deadly precision.

He came up for air only long enough to murmur Jim's name, tip his head back, and come with a damp rush against Jim's thigh. It was the sexiest thing Jim had ever seen.

Griffin leaned his head on Jim's shoulder, his body still moving, but as much as Jim wanted the release, he wanted more to press his mouth against Griffin's ear.

"Iloveyoutoo," he murmured.

Griffin, blessedly, didn't make a big deal. He wrapped his arms around Jim tightly, kissing him again with a fierce might, pulling the orgasm from Jim's body demandingly.

He didn't say anything afterward, but there was no mistaking the huge smile on his face as he fell asleep.

Chapter Twenty-six

Jim spent a week meeting with lawyers. His father's lawyers, the PBA lawyers, the city lawyers. So many lawyers he started dreaming in legal speak by Wednesday.

Everyone said the same thing—Ingersoll didn't have an actual case, it was publicity, and a judge would probably throw it out at some point. What that point was, no one could tell him.

The last lawyer he called was Ed's; he wanted whatever monies were being left to him put in a charitable trust with the projects, all in the Kelly's name, to be decided later. The man agreed. They considered putting the house on the market, but Jim had second thoughts. He paid the taxes for the year and had the handyman board it up against vandalism.

He wasn't ready to let that part of Ed go just yet.

When he was ready—truly ready—he sat Griffin down on the couch and took a deep breath.

"I'm retiring."

"What?" Griffin was clearly stunned; then a scowl formed on his face. "Do not let that prick run you out of the department."

"He's not. This isn't about the lawsuit. I'm just ready to move on. Next chapter of my life and shit like that."

"Is this a midlife crisis?"

"No. Possibly slightly, but in a good way." Jim put his hands on Griffin's shoulders. "I have to warn you, though, I am shit at relaxing. I'll probably be kind of an asshole when I get bored."

"Okay." Griffin mulled this over. "I don't like getting up early."

"I can work on sleeping in."

"Deal."

"Deal?"

"Are you asking me to stay here with you, retired guy? Because I'm saying yes."

"Is this just because you're homeless?"

"No, it's because I love you. You moron."

* * *

Jim went to Captain Trainer and let her know his final decision. She didn't seem surprised. He also urged her to help Terry Oh find another department—because she didn't want the force to lose a great cop.

She promised to help.

He left her office feeling lighter and—dare he think it?—happier than he had in a long time.

"How much time you got?" Terry asked as he returned to his desk.

"Five weeks and I'm out. Need to wrap up some details—Dan Uria is probably coming over to help you out."

"He's a good guy." Terry swiveled his chair. "Man, this is weird."

"Yeah, it is."

"Never thought I'd see you retire on your own, Jim. I thought sure they'd be forcing you out of that chair."

"Things change." Jim shrugged. "Maybe I changed."

"Okay, that's even weirder." Terry tapped his feet. "So...Griffin."

"Moved in. Is staying with me. Is my boyfriend." Jim gave his partner a glare. "There, I said it, it's done. No innuendo or pushy questions."

Terry said nothing but broke into a ridiculous grin. Then disappeared behind his cubicle wall.

"You're texting everyone, aren't you?"

Terry cackled.

* * *

When Jim got home, Griffin was lying on the couch watching a movie. He didn't look very pleased by his choice, but he didn't look up when Jim came in.

"That good, huh?" Jim asked as he joined his boyfriend on the couch.

It took only a second to recognize a very young Daisy Baylor on the screen.

"You wrote this?" Jim put his arm across Griffin's knees. He nodded.

"First movie. Hers and mine," Griffin said morosely.

"Have you heard from her?"

He shook his head. "Jules thinks she might be in New York, but I don't know."

"The paperwork is…"

"All taken care of. Ed's project is mine. Free and clear." Griffin sighed as he sat up and switched off the DVD player. "She came through for me in the end."

"I'm sorry."

Griffin climbed over Jim, twining their bodies together. "Don't be. I got you out of the experience, not to mention I can keep my promise to Ed. That's nothing to sneeze over."

"I'm nothing to sneeze over."

"Not even a little."

"In five weeks, we'll both be unemployed bums."

"Awesome. I'm going to grow a beard."

Chapter Twenty-seven

"So I'm just supposed to pick someplace? Anyplace?" Jim looked at his lover over the kitchen counter, slightly intimidated by his bright smile.

"We can get a map and a blindfold if it would help." Griffin leaned his elbows on the butcher block with a thoughtful gaze. "Or maybe just a blindfold."

"That's not really going to help us pick somewhere…"

"Not *us, you*. You're the one who's retired and free to go wherever you want. Change of scenery for a few weeks, hide from pesky reporters and lawyers, order a lot of room service, sleep late…"

"But you're coming…right?"

"I love when you say that."

Jim rolled his eyes.

"Yes, I'm coming," Griffin said sincerely, shifting his glasses up his nose. That little maneuver was like catnip to Jim; now he was the one distracted from the conversation. "Wherever you want, I'm going with you and taking my computer and I'll be working while you…chase polar bears or snorkel or whatever it is you decide. I have important work to do, and you need to learn how to relax."

"I'm not good at vacations," Jim said stubbornly, coming around to fill Griffin's space, his arms sliding around his boyfriend's waist. "You pick. I'll be happy with anything."

"Then I'm thinking a nudist colony in Hawaii." Griffin slid his own hands into Jim's jean pockets with a squeeze. "I could really get behind you naked in paradise."

Jim laughed, but as he leaned in to kiss Griffin's happy smile, he thought that Hawaii sounded like the perfect idea. Sun and quiet and ocean…

He was already making plans as Griffin's tongue gently touched his.

* * *

Jim cleaned out two accounts and called a real estate agent he found online, giving her very specific details for what he wanted for a monthlong rental as isolated as humanly possible. She promised to do her best, particularly after he included the part about money not being a barrier.

Griffin flew to Los Angeles to finish packing, and then he shipped everything to Seattle for storage at the loft. When they got back from Hawaii, they'd worry about settling in and setting up "home base"—for now, everything was about finding a piece of quiet.

* * *

Terry and Mimi insisted on throwing them a going-away party.

Jim wanted to fly out in the middle of the night like a ninja vacationer, but Griffin forced him into a pair of khakis and a nice polo shirt and hauled his ass to the Ohs' apartment.

Mimi tottered on her heels, the baby belly now grown to a perfectly formed basketball under her shirt. Griffin was fascinated by the pregnancy, hovering close for nearly the entire party to help where he could and ask questions.

"So you're going to adopt," Terry said, pouring Jim a beer at the bar.

"You got happy—stop pushing it," Jim growled.

"Time for toasts!" Nick called, and Jim sighed as he snaked through the small crowd to Griffin's side.

"I hate this," he said plaintively as Heather pushed a flute of champagne into his and Griffin's hands.

"Wah, people love you. Get over it and smile." Griffin didn't have Jim's problems, clearly. He was all but beaming at Jim's side, hushing all Jim's further protestations.

Terry cleared his throat, Mimi at his side. The Heterosexual Power Cabal stood in a semicircle around them like some sort of royal court.

Jim realized he loved them terribly, and scowled to cover his sudden case of the sniffles.

"Jim, we're gonna miss you. I can't say I blame you for running off to Hawaii with Griffin—no offense, honey—but we're going to feel the loss of you here. Don't forget that your friends love you, we have your back and...well..."

"And we're so glad you're getting your happy ending," Mimi added, raising her glass of milk. "You deserve it, don't forget that."

Everyone added a "hear, hear" and took sips of their champagne.

Jim downed his quickly, a burst of bubbles in his throat. He hoped that covered the dampness in his eyes for a moment.

"And we're not going to make you give a speech," Ben called. There was a patter of laughter.

"Wait, he's not carrying anymore!" Nick said. "Now's the perfect time to demand a speech!"

"Have you seen the man in the gym? Don't be foolish, Nick—you can't outrun him." Terry shook his head.

Liddy and Heather announced dinner was served in the kitchen, a table and counter full of potluck dishes their friends had contributed. There was even steak.

"Aw, Mimi—dead cow!" Jim wrapped one arm around Mimi's shoulders. She sniffled damply.

"See? That's how much I love you. You're going to e-mail, right? And call?"

"And come back when Baby Oh arrives—promise," he swore as he rubbed a comforting circle onto her back.

"Okay, so long as you promise."

Ben caught up with him at the end of the buffet line, elbowing him in the side as he gestured toward a quiet corner.

"Uh-oh. Listen, if it's about your Mariners hat, I told you that was a total paper-shredder accident," Jim teased as Ben led him away from the milling crowd of diners.

"I think the season tickets you got us as a wedding present let you off that hook," Ben said, all ducking head and shy smiles. Jim tried to remember when he was in love with that, the illusion of Ben as his perfect partner. It didn't affect him anymore, wasn't a constant ache in his middle.

He was glad he never said anything. He was glad they were parting as friends.

"What's up, man; everything okay?" Jim asked, suddenly worried about Ben's need for privacy and his inability to look him in the eye.

"Oh, yeah. I just wanted...I just wanted to say thank you, Jim. You were a terrific roommate and friend, and I know after I got married there was some distance..."

"Ben, man—married, okay? That's more important..."

"No, I mean, yeah, it's important. But so are your friends. And I want you to know I'm there for you no matter what the distance. You helped me grow up, man. You made it possible for me to hook someone like Liddy." He laughed. "I know you don't need me for much, but whatever it is, I'm here."

Jim was stunned. Jaw-dropped stunned, his hands tight on the filled plate in his hands.

For all those years he pined for Ben, all that time he wanted *more*—this was a thousand times better.

Ben as his friend and appreciating that...

"Thank you," he murmured, sincere and heartfelt. "I don't think I've ever realized what an amazing family I have until this moment."

Ben lit up at the mention of family. His pale skin flushed pink as he reached over to give Jim a one-armed hug.

"Not saying it's in the cards this year, but you *will* have godfather duty at some point. Just don't let your adventures take you too far away."

"Uncle...godfather...I'm going to have to get a paper route to afford Christmas," he faux groused. "Now let's go eat this before Mimi comes to her senses and realizes there's a dead cow on her good plates."

* * *

A few hours later it was just the Power Cabal, the eight couples sitting in the living room among the strewn cups and plates.

"We need to clean up," Terry said, but he made no moves at all. Mimi was curled up against his side, half-asleep but still following the conversation.

"We will. Soon."

"We're cleaning up, Mimi; you are staying off your feet," Liddy said from her spot on the floor.

"Okay," Mimi said, closing her eyes.

Griffin and Jim had commandeered the love seat near the wide windows overlooking the city. In less than twenty-four hours, their skyline was going to be changing for an unknown amount of time. Jim wanted to be close for a little while longer.

"How about me and Griffin do the cleanup? You all have lives to get back to on Monday—while we're on the beach," he said drily.

Griffin gave him an elbow in the side. "Now, Jim, no need to rub paradise in their faces..."

In the end, they all cleaned up except Mimi, who slept away on the sofa, covered with a blanket.

As they put their jackets on and collected the gifts and cards friends had showered them with, Jim made everyone solemnly swear that he would get a call or text as soon as the baby was on its way—and monthly reports from the Cabal's dinners.

"Now he cares!" Heather sighed, pulling him close for a hug.

They exchanged embraces, and no one teased anyone else for coming away with wet eyes.

"Take care, partner," Jim said to Terry; his voice cracked. The other man nodded, blinking away his own tears.

Griffin took him by the arm and led him down to the truck; he didn't even fight when his boyfriend took the keys and drove them home.

Epilogue

Six weeks later

"So how's Hawaii?"

"Fantastic. Jim looks great in a Speedo. We added a few weeks to our vacation, and honestly, I'm considering keeping him in tropical climes forever."

They shared a laugh, and Griffin swallowed back a swell of emotion. He was still a little mad at her, but mostly, he missed his Daisy. And he deeply missed Griffin and Daisy, who seemed to have run their course.

It made him sad.

"How's New York?"

"Oh, you know. Rehearsals are keeping me busy."

He knew she was lying, but it wasn't his place to jump in anymore, to save her from herself.

"How's Bennet?"

"Dramatic and fabulous and never letting anyone forget who the boss is. He's doing a great job with the production. Me on Broadway—it's all very exciting."

Silence lingered for a moment. Griffin watched the perfect blue waves lap at the sandy white beach from the porch of their rental house. Jim was a tanned bronze dot playing in the foamy water.

"I'll be there opening night…"

"You don't have to."

"I want to, Daisy, honest."

"Okay. I'll get you two seats."

"Three, please—Dad's coming down with us." They had plans, visiting up in Albany, then driving down to the city to see Daisy's play. Dad was excited to meet his new "son-in-law," a charming assessment that made Jim go bright red with embarrassment whenever they were on the phone.

"That's…that's wonderful, Griff. I'm so glad to hear that. Three of the best seats in the house, just for you. And a hotel room if you need it—whatever you need, just ask, okay?"

"Just a kiss from the star afterward."

"It's yours." Daisy's voice cracked painfully, and Griffin's heart squeezed. "Listen—I might have mentioned the Ed Kelly project to Bennet, and he might want to talk to you—after opening night, but still."

"Wow, okay." Griffin had a momentary blip of trusting anyone with Ed's script, but Bennet Aames was no Hollywood player. He was an ass, but you could count on him. "I'll set something up when we're in New York."

"Great. I know how much this means to you."

"Yeah." There was a lingering moment over the line when memories and betrayals seemed to sizzle up—but Griffin shook it away. Dwelling would get them both exactly nowhere. "I have a lot in my life right now, and it's all good."

"I'm envious."

"It'll happen for you, Daisy Mae. I know it."

She laughed. "Being a big girl on my own sucks. But thanks, Griff. For everything."

* * *

"How's Daisy?" Jim asked when he reached the porch. He shook himself off like a big fuzzy dog, droplets of saltwater flying everywhere.

"Not great but handling it. I'm kinda proud of her, actually. She's standing on her own two feet for a change." Griffin smiled as he leaned on the railing, ogling Jim without apology. "Need a towel and a hand?"

"Among other things."

* * *

Later on, Griffin got out of bed and collected his laptop, leaving Jim to sleep a few hours while he and the Ed Kelly script sat on the porch for a while. This was everything now. His script and his boyfriend. He'd never felt this way in his life—about a man or a script, he thought with amusement. Technically Griffin was unemployed, no longer owned any real estate or a vehicle, and his savings were just about depleted. His lifelong best friend was thousands and thousands of miles away, and that wasn't just a geographic reference.

But then again, there was an amazing man snoring a few feet away and a gorgeous sunset in the other direction and a script about a hundred words away from being excellent (and he didn't mind thinking that).

He'd take the trade-off.

 THE END

Tere Michaels

Tere Michaels began her writing career at the age of four when her mother explained that people made their living by making up stories—*and* they got paid. She got out her crayons and paper and never looked back. Many pages and crayons later—she eventually graduated to typewriters and then computers—Tere has article clips from major magazines, a thousand ideas still left to write and a family in the suburbs. She's exceedingly pleased every time someone reads her stories and cries, laughs or just feels happy.

To catch up on what Tere's doing these days, check out her website at http://www.teremichaels.com.

Loose Id® Titles by Tere Michaels

Available in print at your favorite bookseller

Faith and Fidelity
Love and Loyalty

Available in e-book format at www.loose-id.com

Faith and Fidelity
Love and Loyalty
Duty and Devotion

LaVergne, TN USA
23 August 2010
194257LV00001B/118/P